SMOKE, FLAMES
and CRYSTAL STREAMS

where two worlds collide

M.T. FOSTER

ISBN: 9798687168335.

To,

Ken and Samir. Good friends.

Table of Contents

PROLOGUE

Take a look at the map and it will give no clue as to where, exactly, the Black Country in central England north of Birmingham might be. There are no borders or specific geographical boundaries to the region, with many traditionalists preferring to define it as simply being an area some twenty miles in length and five miles wide where the coal seam came to the surface. But it is there none the less.

A product of the Industrial Revolution, at the turn of the twentieth century, the Black Country was an inhospitable place scarred by many thousands of iron foundries, forges, nail shops and coal mines, and was described as being 'blackened with smoke by day, and glowing with fires at night'.

The first reference to the Black Country when describing the region came in the middle of the 19th century when a Mister Simpson, town clerk of the city of Lichfield, spoke of visiting the 'black country' of Staffordshire whilst addressing a Reformer's meeting on the 24th November 1841.

The first published reference to the region in literature came in the 1846 novel '*Colton Green: A Tale of the Black County*' written by the Reverend William Gresley, a prebendary of Lichfield Cathedral.

1

Some fourteen years earlier, however a thirteen-year-old Princess Victoria of Kent had written in the journal gifted to her by her mother:

"The men, woemen [sic], children, country and houses are all black. But I can not by any description give an idea of its strange and extraordinary appearance. The country is very desolate every where; there are coals about, and the grass is quite blasted and black. I just now see an extraordinary building flaming with fire. The country continues black, engines flaming, coals, in abundance, every where, smoking and burning coal heaps, intermingled with wretched huts and carts and little ragged children."

Later to become Queen Victoria, with this single entry in her teenage journal, it would appear the young Princess may have inadvertently been the first to give the Black Country its name, the name that sticks with it even to this day.

It was into this hostile and uninviting world that, on 17th June 1903, William F. Cody came with the travelling extravaganza that was 'Buffalo Bill's Wild West'… and it was there that, almost as soon as he had arrived, the gregarious showman second only to P. T. Barnham, had all his cash and jewellery stolen.

'*Smoke, Flames and Crystal Streams*', is a fictional account of what *might* have happened had he later despatched his righthand man back to the Black Country retrieve them.

CHAPTER 1

"Mister Baker" a voice called from inside the horse-drawn carriage that had emerged like an ethereal apparition from the heart of a swirling night mist and pulled up outside the ornate Victorian railway station, a red brick, High Gothic building with a clock tower, impressive spires, gables, and turrets.

Almost instantly answering the call, an indistinguishable male figure wearing a high crowned, wide brimmed hat and long white Slicker – a kind of protective, waterproof, calf length oil skin coat – emerged from the shadows, racing between the station and the carriage, a dark bag slung over his shoulder.

The ground squelched and gave way as a highly decorative, snake-skin boot with silver spurs, sank deep into the quagmire underfoot.

"Goddam hell hole" the mysterious stranger chuntered to himself in a soft, American drawl as he dragged the boot free and the Slicker was splattered with clinging, sodden soot.

The horse that had been drawing the carriage and soon would be again, shook its head, flared its nostrils, and snorted a cloud of warm air, whinnying as the cloud slowly drifted away and dissolved into the night.

The coach driver sat and waited patiently on a hard, open wooden seat with ornate iron armrests at the front of the carriage. He was clutching a long whip in black gloved hands. Shivering, he pulled his broad hat down to all but cover his eyes and turned the collar of his long dark cloak to protect himself from the driving rain and chill night air.

P.C. Oliver Penny twitched nervously, tapped his foot, and wrung his hands as he sat on an uncomfortable bench in the shadowy darkness of the carriage cabin. Wearing his uniform of dark blue tunic with silver buttons done up to the neck, matching trousers, polished black shoes and with a hard '*custodian*' hat on his head, he was proud to be a policeman. Most of all, though, he was fresh faced, still wet behind the ears and had a lot to learn, not least how to remain calm at the prospect of greeting someone he perceived as being famous.

Penny took a deep breath and composed himself, flinched and gasped timidly, almost whimpering when a leather saddlebag flew in through the door and landed heavily at his feet.

A moment later, the stranger leapt in after it.

Ethan Baker was the antithesis of your stereotypical wild west pioneer. Standing over six feet tall, his face was neither craggy nor rugged, but chiselled and refined. His eyes were a deep, disarming blue, and his straight, dark brown hair fell down to his shoulders. Ethan was not so much a ladies man as a man for the ladies and many is the time in some rowdy bar out west, he had been called handsome by some besotted female admirer anxious to make his acquaintance.

Ethan took off his hat, shook off the rain and flung it down on the bench opposite Penny. Ran his hands through his hair as it fell sopping down his neck.

"Lousy night" Penny said twitchily as he reached over and pulled the door shut. "Been raining like this all day. Don't look like it's going to give over, neither. Least, not any time soon".

"In that case you'll be glad to be home" Ethan said pointedly as he flopped down on the bench next to his hat and stared forlornly out of the window.

Penny dithered uncomfortably. "Yes. Right… sorry, Mister Baker" he babbled. "You'll be wanting to get to your hotel, no doubt. Have a hot bath and dry off".

"No need for a hotel. I won't be staying that long" Ethan insisted brusquely.

"But the Inspector told me…"

"I don't give a two penny damn what the Inspector told you, the least amount of time I spend in this goddam place, the better".

He looked over at Penny. "So, let's just head straight for the station, shall we?" he said leaving no room for argument.

Penny continued to hesitate, uncertain what to do. The last thing he needed was to be on the end of yet another tongue lashing from his curmudgeonly superior for not following a simple instruction, he'd been there far too many times during the few short weeks he'd been in the job. He was between a rock and a hard place.

"Or shall I get out and walk?"

Penny was left no other choice than to agree.

"Yes, of course, Mister Baker" he replied reluctantly before rapping on the roof of the carriage.

The driver sitting up front slapped the horse's reins and cracked his whip, and two minutes later they were on their way, headed for the police station on the far side of town.

The railway station was a good couple of miles outside the town itself, and as he sat slouched against its side, Ethan stared out through the carriage window at the desolate landscape. What he witnessed brought misery to his heart.

Someone once said, at the turn of the twentieth century, the Black Country with its coal mines, iron foundries, glass factories, brickworks, and steel mills, was the closest place to hell on earth anyone could possibly imagine. It was a far cry from England's green and pleasant land just a few short miles away, that was for sure. It was as though it was another world entirely, a harsh and unforgiving world, a world seemingly abandoned by God and left to decay without hope of redemption. Even Queen Victoria herself had her valet pull down the window blinds when passing through the region by train, just so that she didn't have to witness the squalor and poverty some of her subjects were forced to live in.

Spawned by the ravages of the Industrial Revolution, it is said that the Black Country gained its name from the black waste that spread mile upon mile as far as the eye could see. The terrain was broken by giant mountains of charred cinders and spoil from the mines. Pit heads, the spoked winding wheels sitting atop them giving them the appearance of a giant spinning jenny, stood stark. Monolithic chimney stacks rose high into the sky, and belched fire and flame into an already polluted atmosphere creating an environment of perpetual twilight. What few trees there were there, were stunted and blistered. Clusters of deserted, roofless cottages built of the dingiest, blacked red brick, were swallowed up in sinking pits, subsided by the mineshafts that lay beneath them, their decomposed, decaying timbers like the demented corpses of damned souls clawing out from the bowls of hell. Steam engines hissed. Chains clanked and the ground shook from the ceaseless pounding of foundry hammers. All day long. Every day… apart from Sunday, for Sunday was the Lord's day, a day of rest and prayer and, despite the depravity they were forced to endure, the people who were forced to live out their lives in this inhospitable uninviting world, were fervently religious.

It had been more than a hundred and fifty years since the onset of the industrial revolution and its legacy was there for all to see.

Penny looked across the carriage at the young cowboy sitting opposite him, his dark brown hair matted from the rain. It was a far cry from the basin cut, the short back and sides worn by most men of the Black Country.

"So, you're with the show too, then, Mister Baker?" Penny finally asked breaking the uncomfortable silence. "Must be something. Quite a sight. All them animals and the like. Spectacular, so I heard".

Ethan ignored him.

"Is it right Mister Cody single handedly slaughtered three hundred buffalo in a single day?"

Ethan closed his eyes, sighed, and shook his head in exasperation. How easily the truth can be exaggerated. Chinese whispers, they call it. The chain starts off quite innocently, a solitary individual relating something they have either seen or read to another. Then, that person passes on the self-same story to someone else, only they embellish the story to make it more exciting, more dramatic. And so, it goes. What was, at first, a simple truth is passed on and on with the same embellishment, until it is blown so much out of proportion it is barely recognisable as the truth.

Penny wittered on, "Talk about excited. I couldn't believe it when I heard the show was coming to town. You could've knocked me down with a feather. Anyway, like |I was saying…"

Blocking out Penny's incessant babble, Ethan continued to stare out of the window. And as he did, so he remembered how it was he came to be in the God forsaken town in the first place. It wasn't a pleasant memory.

8

CHAPTER 2

The Black Country, England, 17th June 1903.

Darkness fell, a blackness so deep you could barely see your own hand in front of your face. It was silent. Deadly silent. So silent you could hear your heartbeat resonating in your chest. Ba-dum… ba-dum…

And they waited.

The sense of energised anticipation was palpable, the almost eerie, spine-tingling silence broken only by the occasional banging of chests followed by a chesty, hacking cough.

And still they waited.

The uncomfortable awareness of expectancy was agonising. A hum rose. An impatience as tangible as was the stony silence that preceded it. Growing louder. Steadily louder. Until…

A burst of brilliant white light. And right there, right in the heart of the dazzling spotlight, was the great man himself, the man they had all come to see… Colonel William F. Cody… '*Buffalo Bill*'.

Mounted on the back of his magnificent white horse with its long flowing mane, Cody had barely tugged the reins before the magnificent beast rose majestically on its hind legs, its forelegs flaying as the showman took off his hat, held it high above his head and saluted the crowd, his grey goatee beard matching that of his hair that billowed down across his shoulders as the tassels of his tawny brown, buckskin jacket fluttered in the breeze flowing through the tented arena.

The crowd went crazy, springing to their feet as one. They clapped their hands, stamped their feet, and whistled and cheered with an enthusiasm way beyond mere excitement. It was deafening. Bedlam.

The visit of Buffalo Bill's Wild West Show to the town had been the hottest topic of conversation for weeks. After all, it was not every day that you got to be entertained by a man who, along with the legendary P. T. Barnum, was one of the two greatest showmen of the nineteenth century.

On the day of the show, people flocked to the show ground, the hoi polloi in their Sunday best mingling with the gentry bedecked in their Edwardian finery. Every one of them lured there by the promise of a spectacular extravaganza comprising of performers assembled from the world over. Cowboys wearing pocketed vests over loose cotton shirts and wool trousers, and with wide-brimmed hats on their heads and oversized scarves around their necks. Native American Indians with feathers in their hair wearing light brown leather leggings and breechclouts - a long rectangular length of hide tucked over their belts - a tomahawk beside them. Or buckskin war shirts decorated with ermine tails and hair. There would be Gauchos, Turks, Arabs, and Mongols, all of them bedecked in exotic, brightly coloured traditional costume. And if that were not enough, accompanying them would be a travelling menagerie of animals, buffalo, horses, elks, mules, and Texas longhorns, a rare sight indeed for people whose previous encounters with wildlife had been restricted to a few scrawny sparrows.

It was a promise not to be broken.

As the lights came up, Cody dropped the horse from its hind legs and trotted from the arena. As he exited, two riders of the Pony Express, dressed in checkered work shirts and with leather chaps over their jeans, raced past him on their way in, heads down as they galloped full tilt towards two poles planted in the sandy ground at the far end of the arena, the crowd cheering them on. Still at full tilt, they expertly guided their mounts around the poles, the hooves of the ponies kicking up clouds of sand and dust before they raced out again.

Replaced by still more mounted horsemen, the crowd oohed and ahhed as the riders flipped from the backs of the nimble steeds, flicking the ground with their feet on one side before flipping back over to touch the ground on the other side.

Even more riders arrived, doing headstands on leather saddles, and performing stunts that, to an awestruck audience that had never before witnessed anything even remotely like it, seemed to defy the laws of gravity.

Next it was the turn of cowgirls dressed in red and white checkered shirts, wafting coloured skirts, bandanas around their necks and with hats hanging down their backs. Shimmering crystal balls were tossed high into the air to be shattered by the sure shots of expert markswomen. Others performed tricks with twirling ropes, the rings of bristled hemp swirling up and down their body and in intricate patterns high above their heads.

A family plucked from the line waiting outside the arena before the show, were driven in aboard the Deadwood Stage, the driver sitting up front on a wooden benched seat, a guard sitting next to him with a rifle resting between his legs.

Several times the stage circled the arena, the faces of the excited passengers beaming as they hung out of the windows and waved enthusiastically to the crowd. Then, passing the entrance to the ring for one last time, they were ambushed by a party of Native American Indians on horseback, whooping and hollering as they gave chase. Riding their nimble ponies bare backed, they had full war paint on their faces, carried lances and had bows strung around their necks.

The passengers ducked inside for safety.

The coach driver slapped the reins and the two horses drawing the stagecoach took off at a gallop.

The guard grabbed his rifle, scrambled up and lay flat on the top of the carriage, firing off shots as the fearsome Indians chased after them, flinging their lances and firing arrows from their bows, the arrows raining down all around him, piercing the wooden coach and hanging there quivering. The driver drove the stage around and around the arena at full tilt, urged on by the cheering audience. The horse's hooves and the wheels of the carriage kicked up sand as they skidded around the bends. And the guard kept on firing. One of the Indians tumbled from his pony and crashed to the ground. Rolling over. Playing dead. Then another fell, and another until the attack was finally repelled and the Indians retreated, galloping away still whooping and hollering, the 'dead' getting to their feet and following them out of the arena.

All too soon, the show was over, and it was time for the finale, a grand parade headed by Buffalo Bill himself. He took off his hat and waved to the crowd. Right behind him trundled a buffalo, a huge imposing beast the likes of which the majority of the audience had never before seen, their previous experience of wildlife being confined to those few bedraggled sparrows. It had long, shaggy brown fur, a mane, and a long beard under its chin. Behind its massive head it had large, humped shoulders, and its eyes stared out from below two fearsome looking horns. Every now and then it would snort clouds of hot air through its nostrils.

Behind the buffalo it was carnival time, the colourful array of performers who, for more than two hours, had so thrillingly entertained their audience waving to the crowd and firing shots into the air. And if anyone thought that the noise couldn't get any louder, they were wrong. The crowd went crazy, wild with unbridled excitement as they as they clapped their hands, stamped their feet, and whistled and cheered their everlasting appreciation.

With the show finally over, Cody strode through the hastily erected campsite of canvas tents and tepees made of animal skin strung over wooden poles, heading back to the marquee that was his home for the duration of the show's stay. It was an incongruous sight, performers and entertainers from nations from across the world preparing their supper cooked on open campfires watched over by the ominously dark silhouette of Dudley Castle, an ancient stone fortification set against rolling black clouds etched blood red from the glow of scorching fires burning in the many factory furnaces that sat below it.

Mingling amongst the colourful entourage, beguiled local folk ambled between the flaming torches and glowing campfires burning all around them, young folk, old folk and mothers and fathers who gazed awestruck as they clutched tight the hands of their children who bounced excitedly beside them and, ever the consummate flamboyant, Cody acknowledged them all with a theatrical wave or tip of his ten-gallon hat.

"Ma'am... Sir..."

"My pleasure..."

"Good to be here..."

"Thanks for coming..."

"Only too glad to oblige..."

Arriving at his marquee, Cody was greeted by William Priney, the valet appointed to attend him during his stay, who stood anxiously waiting for him.

Priney, a slight, dapper man, twitchy and nervous at the best of times, lowered his head and stared at the ground without speaking.

"What?", Cody snapped tersely sensing something was wrong.

"I... err...", Priney stammered.

"Well? Spit it out" Cody demanded brusquely.

"They've gone" Priney blurted.

"They've gone?" Cody frowned quizzically. "What have gone?"

"Your valuables, they've been pinched".

"Pinched?"

"Stolen".

Cody's faced turned to thunder, his veins pulsing, his reddened cheeks puffing out like he was about to burst a blood vessel.

"Ethan" he bellowed thunderously.

Inside the tent, Inspector Hindbuck, a tall, imposing man dressed in a long, dark grey greatcoat and with a stiff bowler hat perched on his head, was searching for clues, opening boxes to look inside them, turning things over to look under them and moving things aside to look behind them. He was a plodder, a sound enough Bobby who was never going to set the investigative world on fire. But you knew where you stood with Hindbuck, and in the fifteen years since he was first seconded to the

Black Country, he had gained the respect of villagers and villains alike; despite his irascible demeanour and hang-dog expression. Everybody knew where they stood with Hindbuck, the townsfolk felt a protective arm around their shoulders, and the villains knew where the line was and not to cross over it. For the most part anyway.

Hindbuck took everything in his stride, so he wasn't fazed in the slightest when Cody stormed in ranting like a lunatic.

"My God, man, what the hell kinda place is this? Cody growled. "A man travels halfway around the world to be here, to bring relief to the folks that live in this hellhole… and his only reward is to be relieved of everything he holds dear".

"Mister Cody, I presume?" Hindbuck said as he stood up from the box he had been examining and offered Cody his hand. "Inspector Hindbuck local constabulary".

"I don't give a damn who you are" Cody snarled shortly ignoring his hand. "Just get out there and find whoever it is that the stole my possessions… or do I have to do it myself?"

"That won't be necessary, Mister Cody, I'm quite sure…"

"That's Colonel Cody to you" Cody corrected him indignantly.

"Sorry… *Colonel*" Hindbuck mimicked. "Like I was about to say, I'm sure the culprit will be apprehended, and justice served on him… given time".

"Time? I don't have time. Two days from now I'll be outta here. And as for justice", he thundered as he

16

whipped a sidearm from the leather holster hanging at his hip and waved it around, "I have all the justice I need right here".

Just then, Ethan hurried in and Cody was on him like a shot. "Round up half a dozen of the best boys we've got... and make sure they're armed. We've a job to do".

Ethan hesitated, glancing at Hindbuck.

"Who're you taking your orders from now, boy?" Cody admonished, "me, or him".

"Alright, Colonel, calm down" Hindbuck said, his tone continuing to be conciliatory and reassuring", "Just sit yourself down, have a drink, and I'm sure we'll have this whole sorry mess sorted out in no time".

Momentarily, Cody eyeballed him, then he hmphed and flopped down heavily in a fancy leather armchair.

Hindbuck nodded at Ethan, who went to a small cabinet over in the corner and started to pour Cody whiskey, his favourite tipple, from an expensive cut glass decanter.

Cody might have calmed down, but he wasn't about to surrender. "So, what are you going to do about it?" he snapped tetchily.

"The first thing I'm going to do is ask you to stop waving that pistol around. There are rules in this country about carrying firearms without a license."

Cody eyed him hard before deliberately placing the sidearm down on a small table next to the chair. "Satisfied?" he asked belligerently.

Ethan handed Cody his drink.

Hindbuck took a notebook and pencil from his pocket and opened it. "So, what was taken, exactly?"

"The whole damned lot, by all accounts. Everything I hold dear", Cody grumbled. "Cash. Personal belongings... Jewellery mostly. My masonic medal, a pair of gold buffalo head cufflinks given to me by The Grand Duke Alexis... and a diamond studded stick pin gifted to me by your own King Edward".

"Must be nice to move in such high places" Hindbuck said quietly and sardonically, not bothering to look up from taking notes.

Cody ignored his jibe.

Hindbuck snapped his notebook shut. "Right, well I'll be off, then. I'll be in touch once I have something to report".

"Is that it – '*I'll be in touch*'?"

"For now,", Hindbuck said slipping the notebook in his pocket and tipping this hat. "Night, Colonel, I'm sure things will look brighter in the morning".

With that he left.

Cody hmphed for a second time and shook his head despairingly. Downed his drink in one and held out the empty glass to Ethan. "I'll have another. A large one".

The oak panelled room overlooked a compound where several black, horse drawn police wagons, the name of the force painted in gold letters on the side of them along with a gold crown, stood idle, the heavy horses that drew them probably comfortable in a stable somewhere happily munching hay. Along one wall,

18

numerous books of varying sizes and shapes were housed on a bookcase made of a similar oak, and on either side of a wide, highly polished desk over by the window there were two chairs, the one nearest the window made of fine leather and comfortable, the other wooden with a hard, straight back.

Hanging on the wall there was a gilt framed photograph of Queen Victoria. Dressed all in black, she looked stern and haughty, much more like an overly strict schoolteacher than a monarch of the realm. Next to it there hung a second photograph, one of King Edward the Seventh. Dressed in an ermine stole worn over a bright red tunic, and with gold chains hanging around his neck, he looked much more regal.

The man standing behind the desk with his back to the room as he stared out of the window, was the 'big cheese', the Chief Constable, a man well renowned for his short fuse and lack of patience. Unfortunately for Hindbuck, he was also the man to whom he reported.

"My God, man, you really know how to fuck something up, don't you?" he said, his voice cracking. "One of the most recognisable faces on the bloody planet and you… you just stand around with your hands in your pockets playing with your balls while some village lout wanders in and… and fucks off with his belongings.

He turned from the window. Short and stocky, he looked like a man who had spent far too much time entertaining rather than out on the beat. Bereft and starting to sound desperate, he glared at Hindbuck standing belligerently on the opposite side of the desk.

"What the fuck were you thinking, man?"

"I…"

"That wasn't a question".

"Why? Why in God's name didn't you stop them for fuck's sake?"

"With respect, I…"

"Don't '*with respect*' me", the Chief exploded angrily jabbing his finger and spraying spittle at his subordinate "All that means is '*shut the fuck up and get out of my face*'. Well, not this time, Hindbuck. This time things have gone too far".

"Yes, Sir"

The Chief flopped down on the leather chair and sat with his head in his hands, his elbows resting on the desk, occasionally shaking his head as he pondered in silence. Eventually, he looked and said quietly, "Now, here's what's going to happen"

"I thought…"

"I'm not interested in what you thought, all I'm interested in is you bringing the perpetrator of this heinous crime to justice.

"Hardly heinous, is it? Petty cash and a few baubles?" Hindbuck pouted cynically.

That was the spark that lit the fire. "It is where my bloody future is at stake and we're faced with a major international incident" the Chief insisted. He has the ear of royalty, King Edward himself, you know that don't you? King bloody Edward".

"Yes, Sir"

"Good! So, just shut the fuck up and listen" he snapped unequivocally. "While you're off doing whatever it is you do all day, I'm going to look for a replacement. Then you'll be out of here. Gone. Understand? Gone!"

"Yes, sir" Hindbuck acquiesced.

It was all very theatrical, and totally unnecessary, and if Hindbuck was either put out or even mildly concerned by the outburst, he did a good job concealing it. Not only had he heard it all many times before, frankly the chances of the old boy finding a replacement anytime in the near future were somewhere between not a lot and fuck all; after all, when he was first seconded there it was for a stint of six months only, until he found a replacement for the previous incumbent who had mysteriously disappeared. If he hadn't found anybody in fifteen years, it was unlikely he would do so now. Not at short notice. Not at the drop of a hat. No, it was going to be a long time before something like that happened, by which time, it would most likely be time for Hindbuck to retire so he really didn't give a shit.

"Now, get the fuck out'f here and do the job you're paid to do", the Chief demanded sullenly. "And do it quietly and without any fuss. The last thing we need is to draw any attention to the sorry mess".

"Yes, sir" Hindbuck replied.

CHAPTER 3

Penny continued to prattle on in the background. "I didn't make it to the show myself", he said barely taking a breath. "I was on duty at the time. Manning the station".

Ethan continued to ignore him. Continued to stare miserably out of the window. The carriage had reached the edge of town by then, and the devastated wasteland had given way to narrow streets lined with begrimed factories and warehouses, their cracked and broken windowpanes thick with dust and grime. Showers of sparks exploded through the open doors of small foundries, the men working inside stripped to the waist and with dirty rag ties around their necks to soak up the sweat. Two at a time carrying cauldrons of molten metal supported between them on wooden poles, across the dusty floor before tipping the bubbling, liquified volcanos into moulds of tamped down sand. Still others, smithies, were working rods, taking lengths of glowing iron from the furnace fire with long iron pincers, laying them on blackened anvils and beating them into shape with a heavy hammer, sparks flying off in every direction.

***

Two days later, Cody had left town still without his possessions leaving Hindbuck to carry out his investigations into their disappearance unimpeded. Nearly a month after that the detective was getting nowhere and beginning to doubt that he ever would. That was just the way it was, stuff like that got stolen, and if it wasn't recovered in the first few days then it would already be too late. By then it would either be melted down for its value or sold off and the proceeds pissed up against the pub wall. Either way, there was little chance of getting it back.

"We might as well call it a day." Hindbuck told Penny as they sat in the station late at night. "Get on home. No point sitting around here all night miserable".

Penny got up and waited as Hindbuck grabbed his greatcoat from a hat stand leaning over from the weight, slipped it on, perched his bowler on top of his head and then put out the light.

They were halfway out of the door when the phone rang. "You go on, I'll see you in the morning" Hindbuck told Penny as he made his way back to his desk. Penny left and he snatched up the receiver, "Hindbuck".

The following morning, Hindbuck was on a train headed a hundred odd miles south to Kensington.

"We received a call a couple of days ago from a local money lender" Inspector George Watson said as he rode in a hansom cab with Hindbuck, "claims some bloke had been in trying to pass off that contraband you've been looking for. Can't say for certain, mind, he can be a lying toe rag when he wants to be".

Wisps of London smog swirled around a gas lamp sitting atop an ornate, black iron lamppost that scarcely lit the narrow side street and the shopfront above which three gold balls, an iconic symbol that has been used since medieval times to identify a pawnshop, hung from a bar.

The Hansom turned the corner and trundled down the street through the haze, the sound of the horses hooves clopping on the cobbled stones echoing in the still of the night. Pulling up outside the shop, almost before it had stopped, the two men jumped out and dashed across the pavement to the door.

It was locked.

"Alright, open up", Watson called, banging his fist on the door.

No response.

He tried again.

Still no response.

He stepped back and looked up at the window above the shop. The curtains twitched. "You heard me, Ezra. Get your arse down here and open this door before I break it down and arrest you for being a prick".

Bolts slid, chains rattled, and keys turned before the door was eventually pulled ajar and a scrawny face

24

appeared in the narrow crack between it and the frame. "Will you keep it down", the face implored, "You don't know who might be listening and I have my reputation to think of".

"I wouldn't worry about that, Ezra", Watson assured him. "Everybody knows you're a two-faced shit who would sell his mother for a tanner. Now, are we coming in, or shall we talk out here?

Reluctantly, Ezra pushed the door open, "This is harassment, Mister Watson, this is. Nothing but", he whined disappearing inside.

A short, scruffy man in his sixties, tousled hair and badly in need of a shave, he shuffled towards an untidy desk at the rear of the shop still grumbling. "You do a good deed and all you get for your trouble is some bobby banging on your door in the dead of the night. Harassment, that's what it is, harassment. I'll just keep my mouth shut the next time".

"There won't be a next time unless you tell us what you know", Watson assured him.

Hindbuck took a look around. It was a dusty, nauseating pandora's box crammed full to bursting with anything and everything. He wandered over to a counter where merchandise sat under a glass lid. Some of it looked like it had been there an eternity. He lifted the lid and looked inside, picked up an expensive watch and wondered how much the previous owner had received to pay off his gambling debts. He put it down and ran his fingers across cheap trinkets imagining what it must be like having to hock that which you hold most dear just to put food on the table.

At the desk, Watson instructed Ezra forcefully, "Right, start talking".

"I already told them what I know" Ezra replied, "down at the station the other day".

"Well, unless it slipped your notice, I wasn't there, was I? So how the hell am I to know what you told 'em?"

"Didn't they pass it on?

Watson eyeballed him bullyingly.

Ezra sighed and took an impatient breath, "The other day some bloke comes in and offers me some bits and bobs. I gave him a price and..." adding hastily, too hastily, "purposely low, you understand. To get rid of him. I wouldn't have gone through with it".

"No, course you wouldn't", Watson snorted cynically. "And did you recognise this little treasure trove?"

"Course I did, in a flash. I can read you know, Mister Watson, and it was all over the papers. Masonic medal, gold cufflinks... and a stickpin with diamonds in it. Some other bits and pieces as well. Very nice too".

Ezra had started to look uncomfortable and kept glancing over at Hindbuck going through one of the cabinets.

"So, let me get this straight", Watson said staring at Ezra unflinching, "Some bloke comes in here fencing stolen property, you give him a price, he doesn't like it, tells you to stick it and buggers off. So, in a fit of pique at having lost out on the prize spoils, you decide to dob him in".

He glanced over at Hindbuck, "And they say there's honour amongst thieves, eh Inspector".

"No. No, Mister Watson, it wasn't like that".

"What was it like then?"

"I already told you... will you stop doing that?" he snapped at Hindbuck, "some of that stuff's expensive".

"I can see that. You got a licence to be trading all this, have you?" Hindbuck asked.

"What?" Ezra said starting to sweat.

"And if we turned this place over, we wouldn't find anything that shouldn't be here – right?"

Ezra wrung his hands. "Course not. I run a respectable business and... Like what?"

"Oh, I don't know" Hindbuck said, taking out his pocket watch and playing with it in his hand. "A man's treasured pocket watch that he claims to have lost, perhaps".

Ezra licked the sweat away from his top lip. "You wouldn't?"

Hindbuck shrugged. Who knows?

"This isn't fair, Mister Watson. He can't threaten me like that." Ezra complained.

"Like what?" Watson asked him. "I didn't hear him accuse you of anything?"

"A man tries to do his duty and..."

"So, this mysterious bloke you claim to have had in here" Watson cut in, "got an address for him, have you?"

"No. Like I said, he just came in and..."

"Right, that's it, then Hindbuck" Watson said with an air of finality. "I think it's time we got back to the station so that you can report that missing watch".

The two policemen started for the door.

Ezra panicked.

"Alright, alright" he blurted.

The two policemen came back to the desk.

"Well?" Watson asked pointedly.

Ezra took a deep breath. "When he left, I locked up and followed him. He's staying in that bed and breakfast up on Bennett Street. Least, he was".

"See, that wasn't so hard, was it?" Watson told him patting his sweaty face.

Priney was hastily packing his case on the bed, Cody's valuable wrapped in a cloth lying next to it, when the door burst open and the two policemen charged in accompanied by two bobbies in uniform.

Priney just stared at them.

Priney was apprehended without resistance, claiming he had lifted the goods on impulse after temptation got the better of him, and, in a fit of remorse, he was about to return them to their rightful owner when the two officers burst in. It was all bollocks. Truth is, he had managed to convince himself that there might be a reward, and he would stand to make more from that than the meagre pittance offered him by the weasel at the pawnshop. Either way, Hindbuck had gotten his man and, in the process, more than likely condemned himself to another ten years of service in hell.

Hindbuck immediately fired off a telegraph to Cody, who by then was with the show at the other end of the country, breaking the news. But if Cody was pleased, or even mildly relieved by the news, he did a damn good job of hiding it. He called for Ethan.

Cody handed Ethan the telegraph. "I want you to haul your ass back there and bring them to me" he growled.

"Says here, Hindbuck is willing to deliver them to you" he said hopefully.

"And you would trust him to do that, would you?" Cody thundered cantankerously, "You would trust him to deliver my valuables here to me when he can't even keep them safe in his own town?"

Ethan thought about protesting but knew it would serve no purpose. Once Cody had made up his mind, it would take the wrath of God to change it, and even then…

The following day he was on a train heading back for the place he dreaded most.

CHAPTER 4

A woman's dainty black-booted feet hurried along the unsealed pathway at the side of the canal, her identity concealed beneath the hood of the long, black cloak she was wearing. She was carrying a small, tattered leather suitcase and was clearly nervous as she started under the arched brick bridge, a dark and uninviting tunnel under the street. She glanced over her shoulder and hugged close to the wall for protection. But the threat wasn't behind her. She had gone only a few short steps before, clearly sensing imminent danger, she slowed.

Further along the towpath, several men were heading towards her. Dressed in coarse, baggy trousers held up by braces, woollen scarves tied cravat style around their necks and flat, cloth caps on their heads, their lighted fags glowed bright in the dark.

Almost before she was out of the tunnel the men surrounded her, pressing her towards the wall of the brick steps leading down from the street, and soon she was surrounded by the lustful, sneering faces of men with rotted teeth and breath smelling of cheap ale and stale cigarettes, their bodily odour overpowering.

One of them, a man with a deep scar and burn marks across his cheek took a last drag of his fag, flicked the nub end onto the path and ground it under his heavy, hob-nail boot. "I bet she knows how to show a bloke a good time" he sneered leeringly.

He reached out to touch her, to violate her and paw her intimately, all the time being urged on enthusiastically by the men standing behind him.

"Give it to her, Chalky"

"Show her what a real man's like"

"Give her what's for"

Scarface took the hood of her cloak, "Come on now, don't be shy. Show us what you're hiding under there".

"Get your hand off me" the woman protested as he made to pull down her hood. "Leave me be". But he would not be put off. She buried her teeth deep in his hand. He yelped and without a moment's hesitation, swiped her unmercifully across the face with the back of his hand sending her sprawling on the ground, her suitcase smashing against the wall and her meagre belongings strewn across the ground.

A canal bridge with wrought iron railing broken by brick-built pillars with gas lamps on top of them, marked the entrance to the town.

As the carriage carrying Ethan started across it, he continued to stare miserably out of the window. Then he

31

saw the woman down on the towpath, on her knees surrounded by the taunting men.

"Stop the carriage" he snapped as he sat up sharply.

"Sorry, Mister…"

"Just stop the goddam carriage"

Penny was about to say something more but didn't get the chance. Ethan, not about to debate the situation even if he was so inclined, was already on his feet. Opening the door, he leapt out with the carriage still rolling, his snake-skin boots landing in muddy puddles in the road spraying filthy water in every direction. He slipped and almost fell, quickly regained his footing and was off like a shot down the brick steps at the side of the bridge.

The woman sobbed, "Please, don't do this. Please. Have mercy" the woman pleaded as she scraped her meagre belongings back into her suitcase. But Scarface wasn't in a mood to show any; not that he had any to show, mercy was a weakness and weakness was dangerous.

"Get her up" he snarled as he unfastened his belt and unbuttoned his flies. "She needs to be taught a lesson".

"No. No. No please. No" the woman continued to plead as a second man bent down, grabbed her arm and began hauling her kicking and screaming to her feet.

Scarface moved in closer, "I'm going to enjoy this" he said with sadistic smile and licking his lips.

The woman whimpered.

He moved in even closer, slipped his hand under her hood, leeringly stroking her hidden face. Then, he started to pull down her hood "Come on now, I can't see your face and you might be a hag under there, and that'd put me off right good and proper".

The woman gasped and held her breath as, grinning through brown, rotted teeth, his bad breath almost unbearable, Scarface stuck out his tongue and started to wiggle it up and down. Leaning in and about to kiss her when...

A dark figure landed on the towpath out of nowhere, a hand grabbed Scarface by the shoulder and, all in one sweet movement, spun him around and flattened him with a right hook to the jaw. The second man shoved the woman against the wall and made his move on Ethan, receiving much the same as the other man as he was sent crashing to the ground, squealing like a stuck pig as he lay there with his hands over his broken nose, blood seeping through his fingers.

Now the others made their move. Edging in. Stopped dead in their tracks when Ethan pushed back his Slicker revealing a revolver, a Colt 45 Peacemaker in a holster hanging from his side. And before they had gone another step, he had whipped out the revolver and was pointing it at them.

"Right, now back off" he insisted.

The men hesitated, defiantly standing their ground, not coming any closer, but not retreating either.

Scarface struggled to his feet. "Alright, all right there's no need to get all tetchy. Were just having a bit of fun, that's all".

"Fun? Is that what you call it?"

One eye still on the thugs, he turned to the young woman who was cowering against the warehouse wall shaking like a leaf. "You okay?" he asked.

She nodded. And as she did, so her hood fell away from her face and she looked up at him through wild, terrified eyes. Like those of a caged animal. Sunken and devoid of any emotion other than fear and hopelessness.

She frantically finished scraping her belongings back into the suitcase.

With Ethan distracted, the thugs made their move. Closing in on him as... sensing the danger, Ethan was snapped from his reverie whipping around and cocking the Colt with a sharp click in one swift movement.

Faced with the barrel of a gun pointing at them, the thugs were stopped dead in their tracks. Ethan eyed them coldly, half wishing they would take one steps closer and he could blow them to kingdom come.

Scarface's face had turned ashen, rooted to the spot as he stared in at the girl, panic in his widening eyes. For a few moments he seemed powerless to move. Then he slowly began to back away, holding up his hands submissively as he insisted shakily. "Alright. All right, no need for anything stupid. We're going".

He flicked his head ushering the others away. They hesitated. He snarled at them viciously. "We're going, I said. Now move it".

The second man Ethan had floored struggled to his feet as, one by one, the louts reluctantly edged passed Scarface and off into the night. And when the last of them had gone, Scarface suddenly regained his bravado. "I

34

hope you know what you're doing?" he threatened menacingly. "It's not a good idea to stick your nose in other folks' business. Not round here."

Ethan watched unyielding as he turned away and trudged after the others, until, eventually, they had all disappeared into the darkness. And when he was sure they were gone, he returned his Colt to its holster and turned to the girl.

"I have a carriage. If you like I can…"

But he was talking to himself, the girl had vanished like a spectre into the night.

"Everything alright, Mister Baker?" Penny called, his head peeping over the rail of the bridge.

Ethan rolled his eyes. Shook his head in disbelief.

CHAPTER 5

A long, straight, tree lined driveway flanked by tall trees that stood like silent sentinels forming a regimental guard of honour, led to Hambley Hall, a symmetric eighteenth-century stately home built in the strict proportions of its Palladian style architecture. Set in picturesque grounds reportedly designed by the renowned designer Lancelot 'Capability' Brown, the hall had once been a residential home frequented by the prosperous and influential, but as the countryside was swallowed up by the polluting industries they themselves had helped to create, the family moved out and the place became a hotel.

At the front of the hotel, was an open courtyard overlooked by the main building with its sharp lines, hipped slate roof, rendered stacks, rectangular windows and wide steps leading to its pillared entrance. Despite the rain, the place was a hive of activity. Horse drawn carriages arrived all the time, their passengers oozing Edwardian sartorial elegance as they alighted them and, sheltering under umbrellas, made their way inside, eager to reap the rewards of fortunes made from the opportunities presented them by the Industrial Revolution. It was a scene of privilege and overindulgence, and a far cry from the squalor and depravity to be found just a short way away in the town.

Where the exterior of the building was austere, in stark contrast the interior was lavish and opulent. Its oak panelled lobby boasted a wide, sweeping wooden staircase supported by heavy beams decorated with dragon sculptures, that led up to a three-sided gallery above. To one side of the stairs, was a highly polished, wooden reception desk where a concierge, dressed formally in a sombre, black three-piece suit, white shirt and shoes shined until you could see your face in them, was greeting customers and residents with a superficial smile, and to the other an equally formal maître-d standing behind a lectern fashioned from the same wood, guarded entrance to the dining room.

Drenched to the skin, a nervous, cowed looking man, Elias Morgan, came in. Wearing a cheap suit, he stopped just inside the door and looked around before heading for the dining room.

"Can I help you?" the maître-d asked disdainfully as he turned up his nose and looked him up and down.

"I... I need to speak to Mister Pyke?" Morgan stuttered fretfully.

"Is he expecting you?"

Morgan looked down at his shoes and shook his head already defeated. "No" he replied.

"Then I'm afraid I can't help you" the maître-d told him tersely, adding as he gestured towards the door. "Now, if you don't mind…"

"Please, please you have to let me see him" Morgan begged, "the life of my wife and kids could depend on it".

The maître-d sighed and shook his head, if he felt any compassion, it didn't make its way to his eyes. "Wait here" he instructed curling his lip.

As he waited, Morgan took a crumpled handkerchief from his pocket, using it to wipe dry his mouth and brow as he looked around wondering how his life had descended to this so quickly, having to beg simply to scrape out a meagre existence. Only six months earlier his business had been thriving, his family was happy and contented and the future looked rosy and bright. Back then he would not think twice about frequenting a place such as this, not feel so much out of place. But now, now that Jonas Pyke had decided he had nice little business…

The maître-d returned. "Follow me" he frowned condescendingly, clearly reluctant at the other man's unwelcome intrusion as he escorted him into the dining room.

Jonas Pyke scraped butter onto his bread with a silver knife, dipped the bread in his soup and sloshed it around spilling hot brown liquid onto the pristine white tablecloth, before stuffing it into his mouth, the soup dribbling down his chin and onto the napkin tucked haphazardly in his collar. In his late fifties, obese and sweaty, his expensive dark, formal suit did nothing to hide the fact that he was nothing more than a slob who attracted the disdain of almost everyone he met, the only exceptions being those with equally thuggish tendencies and corresponding moral values. Pyke owned the majority of the businesses in the town, and almost all of them had been acquired through viciousness and intimidation. There was nothing so low he wouldn't stoop to it. He was not a nice man.

The maître-d led the quivering Morgan across the room that was busy with guests paying through the nose for the privilege of being seen there. It was a picture of refined sophistication. A large chandelier with hanging crystal prisms designed to look like candles, hung from the Rococo ceiling and windows with leaded, stained glass coats of arms etched in the top panels, ran from the ceiling to the floor.

It was a hive of subdued activity as stiff and formal waiters dressed in cut away tail suits and wearing white gloves, their hair slicked flat and parted in the middle, moved silently and unobtrusively between the tables.

The maître-d delivered Morgan to the table and left.

Pyke didn't even bother looking up. "If you've come to beg, forget it" he slurped. "You had your chance and blew it".

"For pity's sake, Jonas," Morgan pleaded, his lip quivering, "I have three children. One of them's only six weeks old".

"You should've thought about that before you started borrowing money, shouldn't you?" Pyke replied without a hint of compassion. "You knew the rules, three months with interest. That was the deal".

"That was before business dried up"

"And who's fault's that?"

"If the customers hadn't been warned off, I might've stood a chance. "But once that happened…"

Pyke looked up reproachfully. "That an accusation, is it?"

Morgan said nothing. Shook his head.

"Good, cos if it was then I might not take kindly to it and then… who knows?"

Morgan stared at him hard. His eyes narrowed and his harrowed face darkened. "I hope you rot in hell", he sneered bitterly.

Pyke was unconcerned, "Aye, I probably will at that" he agreed. "Now, get your sorry arse out'f here and leave me to eat my dinner in peace".

As Morgan turned and walked away a crushed and defeated man, Pyke took another slurp of his soup before calling after him. "And on your way, I would call in and say goodbye to your missus, if I were you. Might be your last chance".

Morgan left and Pyke wiped his face with his napkin. He looked around. Found who he was looking for, Jacko Rawlins, a burly, nasty looking with man a shaved head who was standing sentry next to the door. He nodded and Jacko immediately followed Morgan out.

Morgan cut a wretched figure as he made his way down the darkened street between the dismal factories and warehouses, ignoring the men working there, and those simply passing him by. Instead, shoulders hunched, collar turned against the elements and hands dug deep in his pockets, he hugged the wall trying to make himself invisible from the cruellest of worlds.

Eventually, he stopped at a narrow doorway and looked around nervously, his saucer like, petrified eyes searching the faces passing by. Then, satisfied he hadn't been followed, he fumbled in his pocket for the key to the door, brought it out, opened it up and went inside.

In the dingy office overlooking the deserted workshop below, Morgan pulled out a rickety, hard-backed wooden chair that had seen better days and sat down at the small dilapidated desk and staring blankly. Then he took a sheet of paper from the desk drawer, picked up a pen and, with trembling hands, began to write.

My Dearest, Darling Elizabeth,
How has it come to this? How can life be so cruel as to have dragged us down into this desolate purgatory, to the very edge of the pit looking down into the bowels of hell?

As I sit here, I cannot help but think that this torture is a result of my own failings, that had I done things differently, had I made better decisions, then it might not have come to this.

My Darling, my everlasting love for you and our dearest children, the very thing that has kept me going for the past months, has now become the reason I must end it all. How can I possibly go on knowing that I have brought such bitterness and heartache to your doorstep? The very thought is just too much for me to bear.

All I ask is that, as you journey into a brighter future, as you build a better life for yourself, you remember that I loved you. I will always love you.

Your ever loving husband, Elias xxx

Momentarily, he just sat there, the numbness he felt overwhelming. Then, as though filled with new resolve, he got to his feet and dragged the chair around to the opposite side of the desk. He removed the belt from his trousers. Fashioned a noose, climbed onto the chair, and slung it over a gnarled wooden beam in the ceiling.

He climbed up onto the chair and slipped the noose around his neck, all the time reciting to himself, his voice cracking and threatening to break... "The Lord is my shepherd; I shall not want. He maketh me lie down in green pastures, he leadeth me beside still waters. He restoreth my soul, he leadeth me in the path of righteousness, for..."

He kicked away the chair, and as it began to topple, Pyke's final words to him flooded back to him.

"And on your way, I would call in and say goodbye to your missus, if I were you. Might be your last chance".

In the last moment before the chair gave way and he crashed heavily to the floor, Morgan mercifully managed

42

to release the noose from around his neck. He stepped down from the chair and urgently started out. But it was a cruel trick that mercy had played on him.

Barring his way, his frame all but filling the doorway, stood Jacko, towering over him, staring down at him, fixing him with his cold, empty, emotionless eyes.

CHAPTER 6

The police station stood at the corner of two streets, an unremarkable building with little to distinguish it from the other buildings on either side of it. Apart from the blue 'Police' sign hanging on the wall over the steps leading up to the door, you could be forgiven for not knowing it was there at all.

"And what were you doing all this time?" Hindbuck asked pointedly.

Slouched on a hard-wooden chair next to a rickety desk in the office of Dudley police station, Ethan watched Penny standing to attention on the opposite side of the room. Penny lowered his head and stared at his boots.

Hindbuck, the tall, imposing man dressed in a dark suit, shook his head and sighed despairingly, "I thought as much" he said.

The light from the sign outside shining in through the window, and a couple of oil lamps placed strategically around, filled the depressingly dismal room with disquieting shadow.

Having just recounted events of the journey over, Ethan watched as Hindbuck headed across the room towards a safe in the corner. "What're you going to do about it?" he asked as Hindbuck searched his pockets for a set of keys.

"I'll ask around, see if I can pin it on somebody" Hindbuck shrugged as he unlocked the safe with the key, twirled the dial on the combination lock.

"Is that it?" Ethan gasped in disbelief, "A young girl is accosted on the streets – your streets, and all you can say is 'I'll ask around'. Where's you sense of duty, man?"

"Died a long time ago. Along with hope and expectation" the policeman replied gloomily as he opened the safe door and took out a package wrapped in a grubby cloth. He carried the package across the room and dropped it on the table in front of Ethan. "What did you say he looked like?"

"Big man, dark eyes, bald and with a pronounced scar running down his left cheek".

"That'd be Chalky Harris then". He nodded at Penny, "and seeing that dippy over there didn't see anything, it's just your word against his. And he has four witnesses who will swear you started waving a pistol around before attacking them, and all the time demanding I take you into custody for assault and possession of an illegal firearm".

Ethan stared at him critically.

"Alright, I'll take a look." Hindbuck conceded, "but I don't hold out much hope".

Ethan watched the tall man towering over him and wondered how it had all come to this. He had clearly been around a long time. Too long, perhaps. For the last decade and a half he had, through no fault of his own, been stuck there with no hope of respite or escape and it was all getting a bit much for him. That was clear.

"It's all there" Hindbuck said as Ethan unwrapped the package. "Checked it myself".

Ethan trusted nobody and checked for himself. He counted out the cash and checked the other valuables, jewellery, and other personal items. Everything was there. Just one last item, a diamond studded stick pin sitting in the palm of his hand.

"Looks expensive" Hindbuck said.

"Priceless" Ethan replied distantly, carefully wrapping Cody's belongings in the soiled cloth. He picked up his saddlebag from the floor, unfastened the buckles and opened it. Then he placed the package into it and fastened the buckles back up again.

"Right, I'm outta here" he said getting up.

"Not tonight, you're not!"

Ethan frowned quizzically.

"The storm earlier. Brought the trees down and blocked the track five miles out of town".

Ethan sighed miserably.

"There's nothing leaving here until noon tomorrow earliest Hindbuck continued, "so, I took the liberty of booking you a room over the pub. Nothing much, but at least it's a place to get your head down for a few hours".

"The pub?" Ethan gulped aghast.

"The hotel's fully booked, I'm afraid. The big wigs are in town talking about opening still more factories so they can pump even more shit into the atmosphere. If you ask me, this here industrial revolution has a lot to answer for. One of these days they're going to destroy the very air we breathe... and then where will we be? Still, that's just me thinking out loud".

For the briefest moment, Ethan felt sorry for the detective. What must it be like to become so disillusioned with life? But the dread of spending a night in the pub soon dismissed all that. It filled him with dread, especially knowing that only a couple of hours earlier he had pissed off a bunch of local thugs who, from what he had witnessed in the short time he had been here, would be hell bent on revenge.

"Can't I just bunk down in one of the cells here?" he asked hopefully.

"Not possible, I'm afraid", Hindbuck replied without any further explanation. "But, seeing that you're here, and seeing you have nothing better to do with your time, there is something you might be able to help me with".

Hindbuck led the cowboy down a narrow, dusty, dark passage at the back of the station. On either side were the cells. Apart from one at the far end, all of them had their doors left wide open, all of them were empty and he wondered why the police officer had been so quick to dismiss the suggestion he bunked up there for the night. Not that he thought it was anything but a lucky escape. Six feet wide and just long enough to cramp in a stretcher bed, the walls were thick with grime, the only sanitation a rusty tin bucket next to the bed and the only promise of light the smallest of windows high on the end wall. And there was not much chance of the mausoleum being brightened through that. Even if the light outside hadn't been so defused by the smoke and dust constantly filling the air, there was no way it was going to penetrate the filthy, begrimed panes of a window that was little more than a peephole.

Hindbuck stopped outside the closed door. "I'll warn you now", he said before opening it to let Ethan in, "It's not a pretty sight".

As Ethan moved into the room, the stench caught in his throat even before he had stepped over the threshold. Coughing and spluttering, he covered his mouth and pinched his nose before venturing deeper. At first glance, it was a darkened cell indistinguishable from the others, until he was bombarded by flies that hummed around him and rested on his face. He swatted them away with his hand. Looked up, frowning at what looked like sides of meat hanging from the ceiling. Then it hit him. These were not cuts of meat, they were trophies, scalps congealed with blood and puss hanging by their hair.

Penny jumped up guiltily from his chair as Hindbuck came back into the office with Ethan only a couple of paces behind.

"We were investigating another matter. Found them tucked away in the back of a warehouse down by the canal", Hindbuck said.

"Any idea how they got there?"

"I was hoping you might be able to help me with that."

At his untidy desk strewn with unfinished paperwork, Hindbuck gestured for Ethan to sit before pulling out a chair and sitting himself. "Did you take everybody with you?" he asked.

Ethan frowned, "I'm not sure I follow."

"When you left here with the show, was everybody accounted for? Did you leave anybody behind?"

"An Indian, you mean?"

Hindbuck nodded.

"Happens all the time, not usually with the Indians though", Ethan shrugged. "We roll into town, one of them meets a gal, gets an itch, gets hooked, and before you know it, they're riding off into the sunset without a care in the world. But on this occasion… No. No, I don't believe we did. Why?"

"A scalping in The Black Country? Blackmail, embezzlement, prostitution, incest, extortion, beatings, kneecapping… even the odd body tossed in the canal for good measure. But scalping? Never heard that one before".

"No. No, I don't suppose you have" Ethan said as he got up again, eager to leave before he was dragged any deeper into local affairs.

"You'll get your man, Inspector".

He put on his hat, grabbed his saddlebag from the table and headed for the door. Stopped. Turned back, frowning as he reflected distantly. "Come to think of it, there was one. Not here, a couple of weeks later in Liverpool. A half-breed Blackfoot with a chip on his shoulder. Goes by the name of Dark Cloud".

Hindbuck reacted with curiosity.

"It's a tradition of some native Indians to name a child after the first thing their father sees when they leave the tepee after they are born. It was either that or Dog Shitting"

Hindbuck managed a smile. "And you think he could be responsible?"

"Can't see it myself. Despite what you read in Mister Buntline's stories, Inspector, scalping is something that mostly went on between warring plains tribes. Still does in some places. They're war trophies, something the braves can take back to their tribe as proof of their manhood. But a white man's scalp? Most of the white men were either balding or had short hair, and most of the time they didn't consider them worth the trouble. Either way, if it was an Indian, you got to him before he had chance to finish the job".

"How's that?"

"Like I said, they're trophies, something to wear with pride. There's no pride in wearing something unkempt and matted with blood. They'd clean them first."

Hindbuck reflected for a moment. "Well, thanks anyway".

"Sorry I couldn't have been more help".

CHAPTER 7

Before he had left the police station, Hindbuck had arranged for a carriage to take Ethan to the place that was to be his resting place for the night and for Penny to escort him there. Ethan had protested, preferring to make his way there under his own steam, but Hindbuck had been insistent. Given what had gone on earlier in the evening, the last thing the detective needed right then was for Cody's valuables to disappear again, and for him to be landed with a dead cowboy on the street, he argued.

The 'Elephant and Castle' was a three-storey building built of rusty red brick that stood on the corner of two streets so that it wrapped itself around both of them. It was the community centre of the town, the place to where, after a long day's work in the mines and foundries, workers would gravitate to relax and prepare themselves for the following day's exertion while their womenfolk tittle-tattled and discussed everybody's business but their own.

Boisterous and rowdy, dull, flickering light defused by the customary layer of dust, spilled out through the etched and frosted windowpanes to spill across the cobbled pavement outside.

As the carriage carrying Ethan pulled up out front, he looked out of the window, the discordant sound of people singing along to the addled tinkling of an old Joanna coming from inside. The two men scrapping egged on by a small but raucously whole-hearted crowd gathered around them, reminded him of the Colonel's colourfully exaggerated tales when he was eulogising about his days in the wild west of his youth. All that had changed by then, of course, but the days of manly fist fights, rebel rousing bar brawls and the adrenalin rush of taking the law into one's own hands and either bringing the baddies to justice or leaving them for dead had long gone. If they ever existed at all. Not that that stopped Cody from reminiscing and Ethan smiled as he recalled a conversation, they two of them had had while sharing a whiskey after the show one night.

"*What I wouldn't give to have one last day back there. Life was simple back then, away from all this razzmatazz*" the Colonel had told him wistfully.

Ethan wasn't sure it was a sentiment he could readily concur with.

He climbed out of the carriage, reached back inside, hauled out his saddlebag and slammed the door shut, and as the carriage pulled away, he made his way across the pavement towards the door of the pub.

He was just about to step inside when the door was flung open and a man landed heavily on the ground at his feet, having been unceremoniously tossed out. The man stumbled to his feet before staggering away along the pavement.

"And don't come back again until you've sobered up" the woman responsible for the man's eviction screeched coarsely as she watched him go.

Standing with her hands on her hips, she turned to Ethan and looked him up and down.

"*When you arrive at the pub, ask for Nell Armitage*", Hindbuck had told him before he left the station. "*She's hard as nails and not somebody to be messed with. But deep down she's got a heart of gold*".

Standing there looking at a woman with the demeanour of a sore grizzly standing in the doorway glowering at him, her dark brown hair piled in a bun on top of her head, an apron over her long, dowdy dress that hung almost to the ground and with her sleeves rolled up to the elbows like she was about to challenge him to three rounds bare fist, right then Ethan found that hard to believe.

"I suppose you'd better come in", Nell growled as she turned back and headed inside.

"Whatever you say, ma'am" Ethan muttered to himself before dutifully following her in, eager not to stir her clearly formidable wrath.

Inside, the smoky pub was crowded, men in their baggy trousers and flat cloth caps, women with their hair bunched up and dressed in the same uniform of coarse, dowdy, ankle length dresses. All of them sitting on padded benches fixed against the walls and at round, wooden tables scattered randomly all around the room. Most of the men were smoking, their ale in jars sitting on the table in front of them. The floor was made of knotted, bare wooden boards with sawdust scattered across it to soak up spilled beer. Oil lamps flickered on the walls, and the air was filled with dense, acrid smoke from all the cigarettes that defused the wavering light. And they were having a right old knees up, swaying from side to side as they merrily sang along to an upright Joanna played by an ashen faced, skeletal old man tucked away in a corner near the back of the room.

To one side, a young barmaid, her hair down, slammed a small hatch door shut and went to serve behind the bar. A kid was walking away from it carefully balancing a jug of ale.

"Watch where you're goin' will you?" he complained when Ethan bumped into him and almost knocked it to the floor.

Ethan looked down at a raggedy kid. No more than ten years old, with tousled untidy hair and dirt on his face, he clung onto the jug like his life depended on it. It might well have done for all Ethan knew.

"I'll get a right lampin' from me old man if I spill this" the kid insisted confirming Ethan's thought.

As Ethan watched with disbelief the kid walking out of the door with his jug of ale, a suspicious hush fell. All around, eyes shadowed him as he walked between the bodies following Nell across the room towards the bar. The Joanna player watched too, his hands hovering over the ivories without making any attempt to play them, his eyes wide and trepidatious.

"Alright, you lot. There's nothing to get worked up about" Nell insisted unequivocally. "It's a cowboy, not the devil come to punish you for smiling on a Sunday". She leaned in closer, adding for Ethan's ears only. "I don't go in for all this religious nonsense myself. If there's a God, why would he abandon folks in a place like this? Still, if it keeps 'em happy".

Her words did the trick nonetheless as, almost instantly, the Joanna player's hands were happily dancing up and down the ivories again, and the raucous choir was in full voice once more.

Nell grabbed a key from behind the bar and handed it to Ethan. "Upstairs at the back. Third on the left" she said without the usual pleasantries. "And you might need this", she added handing him an oil lamp. "It gets pretty dark on them stairs".

Ethan took the lamp, thanked her, and headed for his room. And she was right, the narrow stairs were dark... and dangerous... and more than a little creepy. Light from the oil lamp cavorted over the walls creating dark, shifting shadows, and the stair treads creaked with almost every step.

At the top of the stairs, he unlocked the door of the third on the left, opened it and stepped inside

As he took a look around, light from his lamp fluttered on the stark, whitewashed walls. The room was little more than a store cupboard in truth, dark, dingy, and with wooden floorboards that creaked even more than the stairs. Furnishings were meagre, a bed with wrought iron head and footer, a tin piss pot next to the bed, and, sitting on a wooden dresser that looked positively shaky, a cracked crock jug next to a tin bowl. And that was it.

Ethan sighed dejectedly, placed his saddlebag down next to the bed and took off his hat. He pulled back the cover and ran his fingers over the bedsheet. It was pristine clean and shone in the lamplight. Next, he inspected the dresser, ran his fingers over the cracked, brown stained veins in the bowl. He picked up the jug and winced at the dirty, brown water slopping around in the bottom of it wondering if it was safe to wash in it. Even if it was, the revulsion he felt led him to think he might pass.

A carroty red glow shone through threadbare curtains hanging precariously from a cord hung over a small window. He put down the lamp, went over, pulled aside the curtains, and looked out through a layer of caked on grime.

It continued to rain, heavy rain, torrential rain that peppered the ground and rattled across the tin roofs of the outbuildings. Below the window there was a fire escape, and black iron steps that lead down into a narrow, gloomy alleyway filled with deep, dark shadows. Not an inviting place even in the daylight, but at night it was thoroughly unpleasant and positively threatening.

For all that, the horizon was strangely mesmerising. Monolithic chimney stacks belched palls of dense, black smoke into the night skies, the smoke and swirling, churning thunder clouds racing across the sky, etched blood red by the reflection of dozens flaming furnaces burning below. It was like looking into the eyepiece of a colourful kaleidoscope.

"How in God's holy name can folks live in a place such as this", he muttered to himself as he dropped the curtain and headed back across the room, before flopping down on the bed and staring up at the shifting shadows from the lamp dancing on the ceiling.

Tired from his journey, he closed his eyes. But, at first, sleep would not come, defeated by the addled sound of the Joanna and the raucous chorus of people singing that rose up through the floorboards to bombard his ears. All he could do was lie there remembering how much he hated the place and longing for the time he could get back home. To catch up with the show, at least.

CHAPTER 8

Having eventually fallen into a disturbed sleep, Ethan was woken by the clatter of hob-nailed boots across cobbled stones coming from outside. He swung his feet from the bed, crossed to the window, drew back the curtain and looked out.

Thankfully, the rain had finally abated, and down below, in the gloom and the shadow, a steady stream of men dressed in their baggy trousers, collarless shirts and flat, cloth caps, were making their way down the alleyway. No one spoke. Not a word. They just marched on like a regimented army set on a single purpose.

Curiosity getting the better of him, two minutes later Ethan had grabbed his Slicker, grabbed his hat and was hurrying down the fire escape.

Keeping his head down and acknowledging anyone whose attention he happened to grab with a cautious nod of the head, Ethan joined the marching army. Not that he stood much chance of blending in with the background.

Apart from his striking ten-gallon hat, he stood a good head and shoulders above anyone else around.

The procession came out of the yard at the back of the pub and filed across a flattened path of compacted, ebony coal dust towards a squalid factory building silhouetted against the obligatory blood-red of the night sky. Above them, instead of glimmering stars shining in a sea of ebony black, there were ominous clouds and drifting smoke etched with ever changing hues of fiery crimson, orange and yellow.

As they neared the factory, still more men appeared from behind the hills of charred cinders and spoil on either side of the path, their feet kicking up clouds of choking black dust as they scurried to join the throng.

Stepping inside through high, wide, metal sliding doors, Ethan took a look around. It was bedlam, loud, raucous, rowdy, and unbearably hot. Husbands, sons, and brothers pushing and shoving, writhing like maggots in a tin as they jostled for position around a makeshift ring where two men were fighting bare knuckle.

Up in the rafters, younger men dangled precariously from steel girders onto which they had climbed to get a better view, looking down through a choking haze of dust and cigarette smoke, particles of dust dancing around them in what little reddened light shone through cracked, broken, begrimed windows with small square panes.

To one side a harassed bookie was adjusting the odds, taking bets, and writing them down in his book as overly excited punters thrust their meagre savings at him in the hope of gaining a quick return and, for once, putting food on the table.

As the fight ended and the loser was carried out of the ring, Ethan spotted Hindbuck standing expressionless in the crowd and went over the join him.

"Isn't this supposed to be illegal?" he asked as he appeared at the policeman's side.

Hindbuck shrugged, impassively, circumspect. "Depends on your point of view. Me? The way I see it, while they're in here knocking seven shades out of one another, they're off the streets and giving other folks a rest. Me included".

"It's still illegal".

"A small price to pay for an easy life".

A hush fell as Jonas Pyke - short, sweaty, overweight, and dressed in a crumpled suit - flanked by two burly, vicious looking thugs, shuffled in. Jacko walked in front of him, the crowd who parted to let them through doing so without comment or question, eying the fat man with cautious loathing and fear. It was as though Pyke was some devious, imperious senator entering the forum back in gladiatorial Rome.

"Jonas Pyke" Hindbuck said as Ethan watched him from a distance. "Owns most of the factories and responsible for most of the crime that goes on round here. One way or another".

"So, why's he still a free man?"

"Always gets somebody else to do his dirty work for him, doesn't he. Makes sure he has an alibi. But he'll slip up one day… and when he does, I'll be waiting there to catch him".

Ethan wondered if that day would ever come.

Jacko grabbed a three-legged wooden stool, placed it down next to the ring and Pyke lowered himself onto it, the blubber of his thighs hanging over the sides like an exposed precipice. He shuffled, made himself comfortable, then beckoned the victorious fighter to him.

"Nobby Hardacre" Hindbuck said as the bare-chested man in the long johns splattered with blood presented himself to the slobbering puppet master. Pyke gestured for him to come even closer. "Nasty piece of work never, lost a fight. Not that I'm saying they were all kosher, mind. Far from it".

Nobby leaned forward and Pyke whispered instructions in his ear. Nobby nodded subserviently and made his way back into the ring where he waited unconcerned for the next man to challenge his crown

He didn't have to wait long.

There were murmurs of heightened anticipation as a focussed, steely eyed man came out of the crowd and stepped into the ring. Like Nobby, he was bare chested and wearing faded long-johns.

"It's the Tipton Slasher" one of the crowd whispered awe struck to the man standing next to him.

The Tipton Slasher was a fighter with a fearsome reputation. Hailing from a small town a few miles away, he was almost a foot taller and two stones heavier than Nobby and, like him, he had an unblemished career never having lost a fight. It promised a match not to be missed.

Ethan watched as the two men stood toe to toe, eye to eye, unflinching, not even blinking as they sized one another up, psyched one another out. He looked away and through the crowd of men jockeying for position, he caught a fleeting glance of a young woman making her way through to take her place at Pyke's side.

Pyke was growing impatient. "Alright, stop pissing about and get on with it, we ay got all night" he snarled contemptuously in a distinctive, Black Country accent.

The two fighters raised their fists and the fight was on, continuing to cautiously circle one another before the challenger threw the first punch.

"That the best you can do?" Nobby scoffed as he flicked the blow away with no more effort than swatting a fly "thought you were supposed to be something?"

If the other man was concerned, he didn't show it.

Round and around they went, no man wanting to make the next move and be caught out. The Slasher soon began to show signs of impatience and, hoping to catch Nobby on the hop, he made his move. This time, he caught Nobby a glancing blow. So Nobby threw a few punches of his own, the crowd roaring their approval.

Most of the smart money was on the Slasher, so when he became unusually erratic and started throwing wild punches around one after the other, the crowd were rightly suspicious. Something was on the cards.

From then on, it was though neither man could wait to get the fight over and done with, to get out of there. Nobby started throwing punches one after the other. But, unlike the Slasher, his were cold and calculated. A left, a right, left, right, left, all of them hitting the target…

… in the belly…

… in the kidneys and

… to the Slasher's jaw.

The Slasher was taking a battering, his knees already starting to buckle. Rolling from side to side.

A left… a right… and…

As he moved forward, he was stopped dead in his tracks by a straight jab. A right cross and an uppercut to the jaw sent him reeling. He began to sway back and forth, glassy eyed and disoriented. Then he dropped to his knees and with one last uppercut, the fight was over, the latest challenger for his crown out cold at Nobby's feet.

Incensed, dissatisfied townsfolk swarmed around the bookmaker, their voices raised as they demanded their money back. It hadn't been a fair fight, they insisted. The Slasher wouldn't have lost. Wouldn't have surrendered. Not like that. The fight was fixed, they were certain of it. But the bookie was unconcerned and ushered them away. For him, it had been a good night and his pockets were bulging.

Two men dragged the fallen pugilist from the ring. One of them picked up a galvanised bucket and threw water from it into his face to bring him round.

"That didn't take long" Hindbuck shrugged apathetically as he turned to Ethan. But Ethan wasn't there, he'd already gone.

Sensing a confrontation, Hindbuck looked around, his eyes searching the crowd for Ethan. As he suspected he might, he found him elbowing his way through the writhing mass towards Pyke.

Hindbuck closed his eyes and sighed desperately, "Oh great. That's all I need."

The Slasher stood in front of Pyke, Nobby just behind him. Pyke held up his hand to Jacko who gave him a wad of notes which he immediately handed over to the disgruntled pugilist. The Slasher counted it out.

"Don't worry, it's all there" Pyke told him.

"That's us even" the Slasher insisted bitterly as he stuffed the notes into his back pocket and turned to Nobby. "The next time it'll be a fair fight. No pissing about. Then we'll see how good you really are".

With that, he walked away, barging into Ethan who had approached and stood there waiting, as he went.

Pyke looked Ethan up and down disdainfully.

Ethan was distracted, his eyes fixed on the girl. She was not much more than twenty years old and dressed in a dowdy, ill-fitting dress that hung loose from her shoulders. Her dark brown hair tumbled down onto her back and her eyes... her eyes still housed that haunted look of fear and trepidation.

"Can I help you?" Pyke spat.

"The young lady" Ethan replied, "I just wondered how she was feeling now".

"Why, what's it got to do with you how she's feeling?" the slob sneered.

"Following the assault. By the time I got to speak to her to make sure she was okay, she'd already gone and..."

"What the fuck are you talking about?" Pyke growled, turning up his nose and squinting.

"Earlier out by the canal". Ethan ran his fingers across his cheek. "The guy with the scar down his face and the others. If I hadn't happened along when I did…"

Pyke turned to the girl and snarled. "You know what the fuck he's talking about, do you?"

The girl shook her head. "Must have got me mixed up with somebody else, Pykie" she replied, her voice cracking. Pyke turned back to Ethan. "There you go, a case of mistaken identity. Now piss off"

Ethan hesitated. The girl was clearly terrified of the man sitting in front of her and, if that were the case, he had to tread carefully. To say more could put her in jeopardy and he wasn't about to take that risk.

"Something else, was there" Pyke sneered contemptuously.

"Just so long as she's okay" Ethan replied.

He tipped his hat to her. "Miss", and, for an instant before it was gone again, he detected the faintest of smiles on her lips. "Sorry to have disturbed you" he told Pyke before walking away.

Pyke watched Ethan make his way back through the crowd before turning to the girl. "What the fuck were you doing out by the canal?" he demanded malevolently.

Having met up with Hindbuck once more, Ethan walked with him across the cinder path back towards the pub. "What was that all about?" Hindbuck asked curiously.

"Just making sure she was okay"

"And was she?"

"Seems that way" he lied.

"In that case, I suggest you leave things be. No point upsetting the apple cart".

"*And that's it, is it. Wash your hands of it?*" Ethan thought to himself, quietly critical of the other man's methods. "Sure" he said.

At the bottom of the fire escape the two men shook hands, said their good nights and Hindbuck went on his way. Ethan started up the iron steps of the fire escape heading for bed, already starting to get an uneasy feeling even before he reached the top.

Approaching the third on the left, he could see the door ajar. Careful not to make a noise, he slid his Colt from its holster and put his ear to the ingress. Everything was quiet. He gently pushed the door open and...

...the room had been ransacked, his saddlebag on the bed, open and empty. The room trashed.

Minutes later, Hindbuck cast his eyes around. Ethan had managed to catch him before he left the alleyway and brought him back to survey the scene of the break in.

"Doesn't look much different to me" the police officer shrugged sardonically. "Always was a shithole"

"*And you booked me in here*" Ethan thought to himself bitterly. "*Thanks a lot*".

But he was right, apart from the empty saddlebag, the cabinet drawer being open, the bedsheets strewn across the floor and the mattress turned over, not much had changed.

"Just lucky I got you to put the Colonel's valuables back in the safe before you came over here" Hindbuck said with a shrug. "Otherwise they'd be gone".

"Small mercies" Ethan replied sarcastically.

CHAPTER 9

The following morning, after a surprisingly good sleep, Ethan woke early and for the next half an hour lay on his back staring at the ceiling. The events of the previous day still raced around inside his head. There were plenty of questions, but precious few answers. Who was the girl? What was her relationship to the repugnant low life malefactor who owned most of the town? What hold did he have over her? And, on top of all that, there was the thorny question of the scalpings.

Ethan hadn't been as truthful as he might have been on that. The show comes to town, a half-blood Blackfoot with a chip on his shoulder goes missing, and five minutes later bodies started turning up with half their heads missing. A native was involved one way or another, he felt sure of it. And so too did Hindbuck. Still, in a few hours he would be out of there and none of this would be his problem. In truth, it never was.

He swung his feet from the bed and wandered bare chested and bare barefooted to the window. His athletic frame was tanned and his six-pack taut.

He drew back the curtain, looking out on a scene that was equally depressing in the cold light of day as it had been during the hours of darkness. At least at night there were the vibrant hues of colour to brighten up the drab sky.

He closed the curtain and went to the dresser. Tentatively, he picked up the jug, turning up his nose at the murky brown water sloshing around in it. He tipped the jug towards the bowl and…

Nell burst in unannounced. "Looks like I got here just in the nick of time" she said as she shuffled across the room, took the jug from him, and handed him a fresh one.

"You don't want to be using that" she said. "The last bloke pissed in it. Can't for the life of me understand why he'd want to piss in a water jug when there's a perfectly good guzunder next to the bed".

"Guzunder?" Ethan frowned quizzically

"Pot to piss in".

She headed back out. "Nice chest, by the way. I like a bit of meat on a man" she said as she closed the door.

Ethan huffed his disbelief. Poured fresh, clean water into the veined bowl and washed his face.

The pub stood in the middle of the main street in the heart of town. Opposite it, there were rows of double storey, flat faced cottages with yellowed, smoke stained paintwork and grubby net curtains hanging at the windows, and narrow alleyways between them. Outside one of them, a woman was on her knees scrubbing the front step, the sooty faced miners, fags dangling in the corner of their mouths, trudging past her as they made their way home, weary after a shift in the mines, their heavy, hob-nailed boots scraping over the cobbles. Every now and then, to a man, they would cough, hack up phlegm and gob emerald green sputum into the gutter.

Two men stood in a doorway smoking and, further along the street, several women dressed in coarse, dowdy dresses that hung to their ankles, shawls wrapped around their shoulders, their hair bunched up on top of their heads and covered in a turbans made of cloth, stood on the pavement with their arms folded, gossiping in haughty cliques. On the corner children amused themselves, the girls dressed in calf length dresses, ankle socks and serviceable black boots playing hopscotch, the boys in collarless shirts, short trousers held up by braces and with cloth caps on their heads, rolling metal hoops.

Ethan came out of the pub and looked around, it had stopped raining, although that did little to make the place any more inviting. Above him, the skies were grey, an acrid smell hung in the air and the foundry hammers continued to shake the ground as they hammered out their beat. The heartbeat of the Black Country, Nell called it. To Ethan, it sounded more like the monotonous, eerie beat of Indian war drums as they prepared to attack.

Penny was pounding the pavement on the opposite side of the street. Morning, Mister Baker" he called waving enthusiastically.

71

Ethan returned the gesture and as he did so, the two men ground their nub ends underfoot and walked away, but not without taking a quick look back.

Hindbuck had said to meet him at the station at eleven, giving Ethan plenty of time to collect Cody's valuables and get to the station for the noon train. But before he did, there was one thing left he had to do.

He stepped out into the street, nippily stepping back, and waiting as a horse drawn gin wagon trundled past, the horses' hooves and its metal rimmed, spoked wooden wheels churning the ground softened by the overnight rain. Once the wagon had passed by, he crossed the street and started down the other side. A woman came out of a tiny corner shop, cardboard boxes filled with fresh fruit and vegetables spilling out onto the pavement in front of it. Further along, a butcher was setting out the slab in his shop window, filling it with cheap cuts of meat, offal, and faggots. He nodded to Ethan as he passed, and Ethan couldn't help but wonder how, despite the depravity, everyone seemed so happily resigned to their lot in life.

"They wake up every morning in hell, yell at the devil to piss off and just get on with their lives", he thought to himself. *"Those are the cards they've been dealt. Life goes on"*.

He turned into an alleyway and came out in a yard strewn with rubbish, wooden pallets smashed to smithereens, sodden cardboard boxes, discarded mangles, and anything else that had outlived its usefulness.

At the far side of the yard, there was yet another narrow alleyway. Seemed like the place was full of them. Not pausing to look around, he headed that way.

As he made his way down the passageway, he glanced into the tiny workshops on either side. Even in daylight, if you could call it that, they were dreadful places. Dark and oppressive. In one of them, a man sweated as he worked busily. Tempering steel. Taking a red-hot bar from a furnace fire with a pair of pincers and dunking it in a vat of murky water. Instantly, there was a loud hiss accompanied by an engulfing cloud of steam. As the cloud dispersed, the man looked up to see Ethan standing in the doorway.

"Can I help you?" he asked.

"I'm looking for a girl" Ethan replied holding up his hand. "'Bout so high. Dark hair and kinda pretty".

"Ain't we all, mate" the man replied, shrugging dismissively, and grabbing another rod of steel.

"Thanks anyway" Ethan said turning to leave, almost out of the door before the man called after him.

"Hey, mister"

Ethan turned back.

"When you find her, ask if she's got a sister" the man said quite matter of fact.

Ethan smiled and tipped his hat, "Will do". Then he was on his way again and the man went back to work.

CHAPTER 10

Hindbuck paced up and down like a caged tiger, agitated and anxious. He stopped and sighed as he looked up at the round clock with the faded white face and black fingers, hanging on the wall.

It was ten past eleven.

"He should be here by now" he insisted.

He turned to Penny working at a desk on the far side of the room. "Get over to the pub and see what time he left. If he's still there, drag his arse over here".

Penny hesitated, still wet behind the ears and like a puppy not yet learned how to respond instantly to its master's commands.

"Go on then, what're you waiting for?" Hindbuck snapped sharply.

Like one of those new-fangled light bulbs being turned on, Penny sprang to life, jumped up, grabbed his hat, and scurried off as fast as his legs would take him, slamming the door shut as he went.

"Like drawing blood from a stone", Hindbuck muttered to himself as he resumed ploughing a furrow in the station floor, his anxiety mounting.

The minutes passed slowly as Hindbuck waited for Penny to return, and all the time his anxiety continued to increase. What if something had happened to him? To Ethan. What would Cody say. What would the Chief say? The answer didn't bear thinking about.

He looked up at the clock on the wall.

Almost eleven thirty.

The door burst open and Penny rushed in, puffing, and panting from his exertion. And as he stood with his hands on his knees gasping for air, Hindbuck stared at him, waiting for an answer.

"Well?" Hindbuck snapped tersely.

Penny shook his head. "Nothing, sir", he wheezed. "Nobody's seen him. Not since he left first thing this morning".

Hindbuck had already begun to fear the worst, and the worst wasn't getting any better. "Right, come with me", he barked as he grabbed his hat and coat from a rickety coat stand next to the door and hurried out.

Fifteen minutes later, Hindbuck was standing on the pavement outside the pub with Penny and Nell. "You take this side, I'll take the other." he instructed Penny. "And don't take any crap" he added as the young constable sauntered away. "Not this time".

He looked around surveying the street, the grimy flat faced cottages on either side, the corner shop, the miners, the gossiping women, and the kids playing on the corner.

"And you haven't seen him since first thing?" he asked Nell distantly.

"Like I said to young Penny," Nell repeated with concern. "He paid what he owed, tipped his hat, said *ma'am* in that sexy American voice that makes my knees go weak, and he was off".

"Did he say where he was going?"

"To meet you, as far as I know" she shrugged, after taking a moment to think about it. "You don't think something bad could've happened to him do you, Mister Hindbuck?"

"Too early to say, Nell. Hope not".

"He's such a nice lad. Gentle and polite. He could handle himself, mind, I've no doubt about that. Still, he's not like most of the gobby arseholes you get round here".

And with that she swept back into the pub.

Behind the counter of the corner shop, Lizzie counted three sucky gob stoppers into a small, white paper bag, took the two ends, twirled it around until the bag was sealed and handed it across the counter to a woman, Milly, on the other side.

"You got to give 'em a treat now and then, haven't you?" Milly said like she was giving the earth. "Else, what's the point of living?"

Lizzie nodded as she screwed the top back on the glass sweet jar. "You're right there, Milly. They don't have much else to look forward to".

As Milly put the sweet packet in the tattered basket over her arm and turned to leave, and Lizzie put the jar back on the shelf, a small brass bell on a spring caught on the top of the door and rang.

Hindbuck stepped aside to let Milly out, tipping his hat and Milly acknowledging him with a nod of her head before leaving. He closed the door and went to the counter.

"Usual Mister Hindbuck?" Lizzie asked.

"Not today, Lizzie. I'm looking for a man".

"That cowboy. I heard"

Hindbuck knitted his brow. Even after all this time living in the town, it never ceased to amaze him how quickly word spread.

"I saw him leave about half ten. Heading down the street towards the canal and the station".

Hindbuck came out of the corner shop, glanced at the postcards in the window adverting various odds and bobs for sale, and took a look around. Across the street, Penny was in conversation with a woman on her doorstep. The woman shook her head and closed the door and Penny moved on.

Hindbuck started down the street, glancing at the cheap cuts of meat, offal and faggots covered with a grubby net in the window of the butchers. The shop was closed. He stepped around a heavy, cast iron mangle, a couple of tin baths and other bric-a-brac spilling out onto the pavement outside the ironmongers before going inside, only to reappear minutes later still none the wiser.

77

He looked across the street and saw Penny about to knock on yet another door.

"Looking for that cowboy, are you?"

Hindbuck looked down to see a ragged arsed, snotty nosed kid about nine or ten, staring back up at him.

"Seen him, have you?"

The cocky little shit shrugged impudently. "Maybe I 'ave. Maybe I ain't. Depends". He curled up his tongue, licked away the snot dribbling from his nose and held out his hand.

Hindbuck dug his hand into his pocket, brought out a coin and tossed it to him.

The kid caught it and bit on it.

"Well?"

"No, I ain't" the kid laughed as he turned to run… but he wasn't quite quick enough. He hadn't gone two paces before Hindbuck had grabbed him by the collar and lifted him off the ground, his feet flaying like a duck treading water.

"Alright. All right", he squealed. "Over there. Over there going into the alley".

"And what time was this?"

"How the hell should I know? The chain broke on my pocket watch and I lost it" he replied sarcastically.

Hindbuck waited a moment before dropping the scruffy urchin to the ground and giving him a swift kick up the backside. "Go on, get out'f here" he said, smiling to himself as the kid scurried away clutching his tanner.

The police officer and his trusty puppy came into the shitty yard at the back of the shops. Penny started to rummage around in the crap. Hindbuck looked around before wandering over to the back and kicking away a couple of things to see what lay under them.

"Sir" Penny called to him. Hindbuck turned to look. "I think you might want to take a look at this".

Hindbuck looked down to where Penny had pulled out several pieces of tattered cardboard. Under them was Ethan's saddlebag.

"And then there's this" Penny added holding out a shiny silver spur for him to look at.

Hindbuck's face darkened. He surveyed the ground around where they were standing. It was scuffed and scraped, like there had been a scuffle... and his worst fears were fast starting to become a reality.

It was already falling dark as Hindbuck and Penny made their way on foot towards the police station. Nearing it, Penny suddenly stopped. "Sir", he said anxiously as he touched Hindbuck's arm.

Something dark lay in the doorway on the steps outside the station. They edged forward to take a closer look... and found Ethan unconscious propped up against the door, his face battered and bruised, blood seeping from a deep, open cut over his eye and from his nose, blood splattered over his white Slicker.

"God in heaven", Hindbuck gasped.

CHAPTER 11

Finding Ethan bloody and unconscious on the steps of the police station, Hindbuck wasted no time in getting him to the infirmary and the medical attention he so desperately needed. Two hours later, he was sleeping in a warm, comfortable bed having been given a sedative. As he lay there, he seemed comfortable, peaceful even, but the sombre look on the face of the doctor standing next to the bed with Hindbuck suggested otherwise.

"He's taken quite a beating" the Doctor said in a hushed tone. "Severe bruising and a couple of broken ribs. Good news is, they've not punctured his lungs as far as I can tell".

"How long until he's recovered?"

"He'll not be back in the saddle for a while, that's for sure. But he's young, he's strong… four to six weeks and he should be back to something approaching good health".

Hindbuck huffed ironically. "He's going to love that. When can I talk to him?"

"I've administered a pretty strong bromide compound, so I suspect he's going to be out for some time. Might be prudent to leave it until the morning?"

Hindbuck nodded soberly.

When Hindbuck returned the following morning, a pretty young nurse had just finished wrapping Ethan's ribs in bandage. She tied off the bandage, plumped up his pillows and made him comfortable. He groaned and closed his eyes.

"I'll come back later and make sure you're comfortable" the nurse said before leaving.

"Thanks, miss" Ethan managed politely.

As she bustled out, Hindbuck couldn't help but notice the young woman's cheeks had visibly reddened. He half smiled and shook his head, wondering what it was that was so alluring about the American accent... or his naked torso, for that matter.

Ethan opened his eyes and forced a smile, making light. "Guess I missed the train, then?" he said painfully.

"'Fraid so. How're you feeling?"

"I've been better. When can I get outta here?"

"You'll have to ask the Doc about that one. Can you remember what happened?"

"Some".

He paused to draw an agonising breath, holding his hand to his ribs, before continuing. "I had eggs and beans for breakfast, paid Nell what I owed, said so long to her and headed off to meet up with you at the jailhouse".

He coughed, clearly finding it hard to breath. Then he continued, "I left the pub 'bout ten, in plenty of time to get to you and then on to the railroad station in time for the noon train. Least that's what I thought.

"And?"

"I took a look down one of those alleyways with all the workshops, I was just crossing back through the yard at the rear of the shops, when I was set upon by half a dozen men".

"Did you recognise any of them?"

"Hardly, one man looks the same as the next to me the way they dress. Besides, it all happened so fast".

"Anything else?"

Ethan shook his head weakly. "One minute there were heavy boots raining down on me, the next I woke up in here. I guess it must have been those guys from the other night looking for revenge after spoiling their fun".

"Maybe… may not" Hindbuck pondered thoughtfully before suddenly brightening. "Right, I'll get out of here and leave you in peace. We'll talk later".

Ethan nodded and closed his eyes.

Hindbuck opened the door to leave.

The young woman Ethan had rescued from her attackers was standing in the doorway blocking his way. Clearly nervous and hesitant about coming in, she lowered her eyes from him.

Hindbuck glanced at Ethan lying in the bed with his eyes closed, and then back to her. "Make it quick, he needs his rest" he said.

The young woman nodded, and he left.

On his walk back to the police station, Hindbuck pondered his next move. Ethan had been beaten to within an inch of his life and then delivered anonymously to the station. But why?

Perhaps some good Samaritan had stumbled upon him unconscious, delivered him to the station, found the place unmanned and dumped him on the steps.

Unlikely! So, what then?

Maybe he had crawled there from wherever it was he had been assaulted and passed out in the porch. But Hindbuck had checked the pavement and there was no blood, surely there would have been blood if he had managed to drag himself there. Besides, he would have been in no fit state to drag himself anywhere.

No, it was a veiled message of some sort, he was sure of it... and every instinct was telling him Pyke was involved. He just had to figure out how, and why.

The young woman had clearly made an effort to impress. Her dark brown hair that had hung loose, was now tied back in a ponytail, and her eyes had regained some of their sparkle. She was wearing her Sunday best, a pretty but still cheap floral cotton dress that was far too light for the time of year. She was carrying a small purse which she clutched in front of her with both hands. Like it was her comfort blanket.

She made her way to Ethan's bedside and finding him sleeping, stood looking down at him. She was about to leave again when he woke, looked up and forced a weak smile.

"I heard what happened and..." She hesitated and looked away before continuing. "I just wanted to thank you, that's all. It's not every day somebody stands up to the bullies. Not round here".

"You're welcome. Pleased to be of service" Ethan assured her weakly.

As he watched her waiting for her to say something more, he couldn't help thinking she was not the frightened child he first thought, that she was simply a young woman defeated by the life she had been forced to endure.

"I'm sorry, I have to go" she said. "If he finds out I was here, he'll...", her words petered away.

"He? You mean, Pyke?"

The young woman's empty eyes flicked away, as she bit her lip, close to tears.

"I have to go" she said starting for the door.

Ethan called after her, "Miss".

She turned and looked back.

"I don't even know your name".

"Ella... Ella Hardcastle" she said before walking out and closing the door behind her.

Some people talk about a theatre of dreams, but Pyke's lair was no theatre of dreams, it was an auditorium of violence and intimidation. A place of nightmares.

Sitting anonymously next to an open workshop down near the canal basin, the dilapidated warehouse with its shattered and cracked windowpanes appeared abandoned and derelict, indistinguishable. And that was just the way Pyke liked it, the anonymity leaving him plenty of room to plot his many delinquencies and wrongdoings without outside interference.

Hindbuck had thought hard and long before venturing into Pyke's sleazy world. He knew of the place, of course he did, although he rarely ventured there, and those who did weren't about to admit it. Apart from those closest to him, entry was strictly by invitation only and, if you received such an unwelcome invitation, it was usually to have your finger nails plucked, or to be given a severe warning that, should you not toe the line in future, punishment would be much more excruciating and probably involve a loss of blood… or worse, even.

Hindbuck knew all this, but he didn't lose much sleep over it. Why should he? The invitees were invariably felons who had committed some heinous crime against society and given his limited manpower and resources, half of them would walk away scot free but for Pyke's kangaroo court. He didn't like it, he didn't like it one little bit, but that was the way it was. At least the bad men were getting their comeuppance. Even so, there was a line, and if somebody overstepped that line…

He strode purposefully through particles of dust dancing in the dull light that spilled through the dirty high windows and spread out across the floor of the uninviting warehouse, heading for an iron staircase leading up to the dilapidated, ramshackle of an office from which Pyke was able to survey all from above; the disgusting rat's nest.

The less than lugubrious office that was the centre of the overlord's subversive operations was as dark, and as dirty as the warehouse below it, with finely spun cobwebs hanging in every high corner. A battered and cracked wooden filing cabinet that rested against the wall was covered in a thick layer of dust, as was the wide window that looked out over the warehouse floor. Next to the cabinet, equally dusty, faded and battered cardboard boxes were stacked three high. All this watched over by an incongruous black and white picture of a stern and disapproving Queen Victoria hanging at an obscure angle on the wall.

Wedged pugnaciously in a carver chair, folds of flabby fat leaching between the arm rests, Pyke was reading the riot act to three of his heavies, Billy Pearce, Tommy Smith, and Abel Edwards, who were assembled before him like naughty schoolboys standing before their ogre of a headmaster. As he ripped the shit out of them, spittle flew from his slapping jowls that hung lower than those of the Staffordshire bull terrier sitting at his feet. Every now and then he would thump the table causing clouds of dust to drift in the already polluted air.

Hearing the sound of footsteps on the stairs, Pyke paused and narrowed his eyes, frowning quizzically.

The dog jumped to its feet and started to bark.

Pyke kicked it viciously and heartlessly sending it whimpering into the corner.

As the footsteps grew closer, Pyke nodded to Jacko who was sitting next to him. Jacko got up, crossed the room, and opened the door.

Hindbuck stood impassive in the doorway, his hands dug deep in the pockets of his greatcoat, his bowler hat on his head. He didn't display any hint of apprehension, even though deep down he felt it. It didn't do to show weakness. Not where Pyke was concerned.

Pyke smiled disingenuously. "Ah, Neville, what took you so long? I was expecting you sooner."

Inside, Hindbuck bristled, he didn't like being called by his first name, especially not by a low life such as Pyke. He stepped over the threshold and watched guardedly as Pyke nodded a silent but menacing threat to his cohorts who scarpered out of the door immediately. Apart from the ever present Jacko who never left his side. Secretly, they were thankful the police officer had arrived when he did, and they were spared further admonishment.

"Come to give thanks, have you, Neville?" Pyke smirked smarmily.

"Thanks for what?"

"Delivering that pretty boy Yankee of yours safe and sound. Well... not exactly sound, I admit, but safe nonetheless."

He struggled to his feet and lumbered slovenly to the cabinet in the corner. "When my blokes came and told me what they'd found, I thought to myself, *Neville would want to know about this*. And looks like I was right."

"Your men found him?"

"In the backyard of the shops. Somebody had given him a right goin' over, from what I hear". Pyke was revelling in his moment of glory. It wasn't often he got one over on Hindbuck and he was going to make the most of it. "So, I had them deliver him to you sharpish. So he could get medical attention. Kind of me, wasn't it?"

Hindbuck had been caught off guard. Pyke playing the Good Samaritan didn't sit right. On the other hand if he was telling the truth…?

"You expect me to believe that?" he asked.

"Believe what you like. It's the truth either way round". He opened the cabinet drawer and took out Ethan's Colt, "and, as a sign of good faith, you might want to return this to him".

He held the Colt out to Hindbuck.

"He must've dropped it when whoever it was that was responsible jumped him".

Hindbuck hesitated before he took the pistol from him. He said nothing, just frowned curiously.

"Ay I goin' to get a thank you, Neville?" Pyke asked smirking superciliously.

CHAPTER 12

"I went to see Pyke", Hindbuck said as he handed Ethan the Colt and the cowboy put it down on the bed next to him.

"You think he was the one who delivered me back to the station?" Ethan asked.

"So he says" Hindbuck nodded

He took a moment to think it through. "He's up to something, I know he is. I just haven't figured out what".

"And what about the man from the other night, the one that led the attack on the girl?"

"Chalky Harris?" Hindbuck shook his head. "No luck, I'm afraid. Seems like he's done a disappearing act. Keeping his head down. Either that or Pyke's found out and he's suffering for it".

"You have any proof of that?"

"I don't need proof. Not where Pyke's concerned".

For a few minutes, the two men sat quietly, Hindbuck trying to make sense of it all, Ethan trying to remember anything significant.

It was Ethan who finally broke the silence.

"Supposing it wasn't Pyke who put me in here and this other man wasn't the one who attacked me" he said thoughtfully. "There is another who might have a grudge... the boxer from the other night"

"Nobby?"

Ethan nodded.

"He threatened you? When?"

"When we were last here with the show".

***

A string of men, locals, lined up outside the wooden door to one of the factory units, all of them dressed in the same uniform of baggy trousers, collarless shirts, and flat cloth claps. Most of them were smoking, their rasping coughs issuing thick, green phlegm they spat onto the ground.

A wrangler, Tom Carter, came out from inside and announced, "Right, in you come".

The men took one last drag of the coffin nails that, along with the polluted air they were forced to breath every day, were leading them to an early death, and ground the nubs under foot before following him inside.

On the promise of an honest day's work, the men formed an orderly a line leading to a small table where Ethan sat waiting. In front of him a list of hands they might need to help out while the show was in town.

Carter sat down next to him, and for the next few minutes Ethan either shook his head or nodded his approval as, one by one, the men came to the table. Some of them left disappointed, others left dockets handed to them by Carter with the same curt instruction, "Be at the showground at eight o'clock sharp. Later than that, don't bother".

Nobby and three equally thuggish looking men arrived outside, walked straight past the men waiting patiently in line and headed inside. No one complained, no one dared. That was just the ways things were unless, of course, you wanted to get on the wrong side of the bare-knuckle pugilist. And nobody wanted to get Nobby's wrong side, least, not if they knew what was good for them.

Ethan nodded to Carter who immediately stood and began ushering the men away. "Thank you, gentlemen, that will be all for today".

As the men filed away muttering their disappointment, Nobby approached the table with his cohort. "Right, where do we sign?" he asked bluntly.

"Sorry, we have all the men we need", Ethan said absent mindedly, not bothering to look up from the forms he was filling out.

"Then, scratch their names out and put ours in"

"Sorry, I can't do that".

"Can't... or wont?"

Ethan looked up at him. Then back down at his papers. "If you wanted work, you should have gotten here earlier. Now, if you don't mind".

The atmosphere changed in an instant, the disappointed murmuring of the rejected men abating in a moment as they shared looks with one another waiting for the bomb to go off.

"I don't think you understand. It don't work like that round here" Nobby said menacingly. "We take first dibs and the rest take what's left. Understand".

"I understand completely. You're a vicious bully and folks are too afraid to stand up to you. But things don't work that way where I hail from".

Ethan continued with his paperwork.

Nobby eyed him threateningly. "You're going to regret you said that", he assured him.

"I doubt that" Ethan replied unconcerned.

Momentarily, Nobby continued to eyeball the cowboy. Then he spun on his heels, the crowd of men parting to let him through as he marched away with his cohort in tow.

***

"Yes, well I can see how that might upset him, and he does have a long memory", Hindbuck said philosophically. "Even so, I'm not sure what I can do about it without proof".

"*Even if you had the inclination*" Ethan thought to himself cynically, not having the chance to say as much before they were disturbed by a commotion outside.

"You can't go in there" the nurse could be heard to say. "He's a sick man and…"

"I can do what I damned well like" the gruff voice of Cody assured her

A moment later, the door burst open and Cody charged in, the pretty nurse tagging along in his wake.

"I'm sorry about this, sirs", she said clearly flustered and uncertain.

"You can be just as sorry outside" Cody told her caustically, taking her by the arm to usher her out. The nurse stood her ground, looking to Hindbuck for support. Hindbuck simply nodded to her and, eyeing Cody down her nose with contempt, she left.

Cody slammed the door shut behind her, then turned to Hindbuck, glaring at him accusingly.

"Well? What the hell happened? Why's my best man lying in a hospital bed looking like he's been savaged by a pack of rabid prairie dogs?"

Immediately after delivering Ethan to the infirmary, Hindbuck had managed to get hold of Cody - who by then was camped hundreds of miles away at the other end of the country - by telephone and filled him in briefly on what had happened. The conversation was heated to say the least and had ended with Hindbuck assuring Cody he would do everything in his power to bring the guilty party to justice and promising to keep Cody informed. But such an assurance, no matter how sincerely it was given, wasn't sufficient for Cody, and immediately the show was finished that night, he headed back to the Black Country to check on the condition of his right-hand man.

Once he had calmed down, between them Ethan and Hindbuck filled Cody in on the details of the assault, and when they were done, Hindbuck repeated his assurance that no stone would be left unturned in the pursuit of the assailant. Cody wasn't entirely satisfied. He was used to decisive, instant action, even if that did mean ruffling a few innocent feathers along the way. But it seemed like he had no choice other than to trust in the efforts of the local policeman. But not without one last warning.

"If you can't get the job done, I'll do it myself. Understand? I'll round up a posse and make sure the perpetrators are put behind bars where they belong" he snapped emphatically.

Hindbuck nodded, but deep down inside he was thinking to himself, "*If only it was that easy. You don't know the Black Country*".

CHAPTER 13

Leaving Ethan to get some much-needed sleep, it was dusk by the time Hindbuck and Cody had made the short walk back to the police station. Cody, having made the decision to leave things in the policeman's hands for now, insisted on collecting his valuables and then catching the next train out of there. He had a show to perform the following night and his adoring public couldn't be kept waiting. Not for anything.

Hindbuck put the key in the lock of the safe and twirled the combination, took out Cody's valuables wrapped in the grubby cloth and handed them to him. "It's all there", he assured him.

"Thanks. Very much appreciated" Cody replied stuffing the package inside his tassled jacket. "Can I ask you something?"

"Ask away".

"How do you live in a place like this? The constant lack of sunshine, the people, the lawlessness… doesn't it get you down?"

"Sometimes".

"It was bad enough out west, but at least if a man was going to shoot you, he didn't have to wait until your back was turned".

Hindbuck reacted defensively. "You have to understand, Colonel, the majority of folks that live around here are salt of the earth. God fearing folks with a caustic sense of humour who work hard during the week and give thanks for what they have on a Sunday. It's not a lot, I know, but what they do have, they're grateful for. As for the few that break the law, most of them do so through fear and intimidation, careful not to get their hands dirty in the process. Knowing they're there, is one thing. Tying them down to anything… that's another".

"Like I said on the walk back" Cody responded after a few moments consideration, "need any help, just let me know and I can be back here in no time with all men you need. Good men. Loyal men".

"I'll bear that in mind" Hindbuck nodded.

Five minutes later, the two men were standing on the pavement outside the station saying their goodbyes. They shook hands and walked away in opposite directions, Cody heading for the station, Hindbuck heading for home.

As he sauntered along the street with his hands in his pockets, Hindbuck got to thinking about what Cody had said. Maybe he was right, maybe he did need help in cleaning up the town, leaving his mark before he retired and walked off into the sunset. If he could find the sunset, that is. It had been so long since he last saw it, he'd forgotten what it looked like.

"Hindbuck"

Hindbuck turned back to see Cody further down the street looking back at him. "I have some time to kill before my train leaves. Can I buy you a drink?"

Hindbuck hesitated a moment before walking back.

Hindbuck sat in The Elephant and Castle nursing a pint of black and tan, leaning back on one of the benches and wondering if Cody ever switched off.

Cody was at the bar entertaining the customers with tales of wild west daring and adventure and posing for photographs taken by a photographer from the local newspaper. Just how the plucky reporter had got there so quickly was anybody's guess. It had been quiet when they first arrived, but once news spread that Buffalo Bill was holding court in the pub, folks started arriving in droves. It was only reasonable the news wouldn't take long to get through to the press, he supposed. No matter.

Hindbuck looked over to see Nobby sitting right at the back of the room with his equally thuggish looking mates, Frankie, and wondered if he should go over and confront him, and what good it might do if he did.

Cody was waxing lyrical, playing to the crowd, "And then there was the time a few years back when Annie Oakley, *The Rifle Queen*, was with the show - now there's a gal, could take a rabbits brain out through its ass without it even noticing".

There was a sharp intake of breath accompanied by wide eyes. Then stifled laughter.

"So, when the performance done", Cody continued, "we were granted a reception and Victoria was so taken by Annie's sharpshooting, she asked to meet her."

"Queen Victoria?" asked one of the punters, jaw dropping. More wide eyes.

"The very same. A close friend at the time. Dead now, of course, God rest her soul".

Hindbuck shook his head, wondering at how easily the names of the rich and famous just fell off Cody's tongue. He glanced over to where Nobby was sitting with his Frankie. Then he took a swig and got up.

"Anyways", Cody continued, "when I introduced them, Victoria took Annie's two hands in her own like this", he took Nell's hands and held them tight, all the time gazing into her eyes with mock admiration. "And you know what she said?"

The punters shrugged and shook their heads, hanging onto his every word.

"You're a very, very clever little girl".

There was laughter all round.

Nobby looked up to see Hindbuck standing over him. "Well, if it isn't Mister Plod, the local Bobby" he said snidely. "Come to see if we had anything to do with the assault on that cowboy, have you?"

"And did you?"

"Wouldn't tell you if I did? But, as it happens, no. Not that I'm sorry. Too cocky by half, that one. Don't stick to the rules. Now, if you don't mind, piss off and leave me to enjoy my drink in peace... unless, of course, you have something to tie me to and have evidence to prove it".

Hindbuck stared at him coldly.

Cody posed for yet another photograph, his arm around Nell at the bar. And after the flash had gone off, he said to her without even the slightest hint of modesty. "You hang that there photograph over the bar, Nell, and if you take good care of it, it will still be hanging there when the next century comes around. A reminder of the day Buffalo Bill Cody came to town".

Nel glanced at him sideways... cocky bugger!

A horse-drawn carriage, its driver sitting up front on the usual hard, wooden seat, waited in the shadows on the darkened street outside Elias Morgan's factory.

Inside, in the small office upstairs, the overturned chair was still lying on the floor. Pyke picked it up and plonked it down next to the desk, flopped down on it, picked up a ledger from the desk and started flicking through the pages.

Standing opposite him, Morgan's wife was clearly distressed, tears streaming down her face as she clutched a young baby to her chest with one hand and held tight the hand of the small girl standing next to her.

Pyke looked up as Jacko came in and nodded to him. He snapped the ledger shut with a sharp crack. "Right, that's it then", he said lumbering to his feet. "Everything seems to be in order. You have until the end of Friday to clear out your things… understood?"

"For God's sake, Jonas", Morgan's wife pleaded, "Have some mercy".

"Mercy? Did your old man have any mercy when he borrowed money off me and then topped himself to avoid paying it back?"

The woman looked away.

"No, I thought not".

Pyke looked down at the girl. She was about ten years old with wide, innocent blue eyes and flaxen hair that tumbled down across her shoulders in ringlets.

"Pretty little thing, ay she?" he said through slobbering jowls. "She's goin' to be showing some bloke a good time before long". He looked the woman in the eye. "Perhaps we can work something out".

The woman glared at him with utter loathing and contempt as she spat at him, "Don't you dare touch her. Touch her and I swear I'll…"

"What? You'll swing for me?"

The woman didn't reply.

"I didn't think so".

He ran his podgy, sweaty fingers through the girl's hair. Kissed them and pressed them to her lips. The girl recoiled and her mother slapped his hand away.

Pyke glared at her. "That'll be Thursday four o'clock then" he told her.

He kissed the top of girl's head and headed for the door, calling back, "And don't leave anything behind, or I'll take that an' all" as he shambled out.

The woman was devastated. She started to shake. Fighting to breathe. Life as she knew it had just ended, walked out of the door leaving her with nothing.

She began to sob uncontrollably.

"You tell a good story, I'll say that", Hindbuck said before taking a swig of his beer. Cody sat down next to him. Glanced over towards the bar and then back again. "All that nonsense? Promotion, Hindbuck, promotion. Total crock of shit for the most part".

If Hindbuck was in any way surprised, he certainly didn't show it. "You're saying the stories put around about you are not true?"

"Hell, no. Met the writer of dime novels one day, a fella named Ned Buntine, we got talking and next thing you know there was an article about me appearing in the *New York Weekly*. From then on, the stories, mostly dreamed up by Buntline himself, I might add, just kept on coming. Not that I'm complaining, I've done well out of them".

"And the buffalo?"

"Did I slaughter more than four thousand of the beasts, you mean?"

Hindbuck nodded.

"I was contracted by the *Kansas Pacific Railway* to supply food for their workers, so I wasn't really counting. All I can say is... they were well fed".

"And that's when you got the nickname?

"Buffalo Bill?"

Hindbuck nodded for a second time.

"There was another fella, part Cheyenne, who went by the name of Comstock. He was claiming the name for himself... so we had a shooting match to determine who had the exclusive right to it. I won".

He grabbed his whiskey from the table and downed it in one. "Anyways" he said, "Much as I'd like to stay here chewing the fat all night, I have a train to catch. Take care of him, Hindbuck. Make sure he comes back safe. That boy's like a son to me and if anything should happen to him... hell, just listen to me chattering on like an old maid. Just take care of him, that's all I ask".

Hindbuck nodded.

Cody got up and tipped his wide brimmed hat. "See you around, partner. And remember what I said. You need any support, you know where to find me".

And with that, he was gone.

Almost.

It took him nearly ten minutes to get out of the pub by the time he had said his goodbyes and shaken hands with all the well-wishers.

CHAPTER 14

After a few days, Ethan was discharged from hospital with the express instruction that he rest up and not undertake anything physical until his ribs had knitted. He had been quick to agree to the terms but had no intention of actually carrying them out. But there was one thing he hadn't accounted for in the equation... Nell.

On leaving hospital, Nell had insisted he move back into the tiny room over the pub where she could keep an eye on him, and if he thought Cody was a hard task master, Nell was something else.

Apart from popping in every five minutes to refresh his water jug and plump up his pillows, she made damned sure he was well fed.

"You need to build up your strength" she would say to him as she sat him up in bed and placed a bowl of soup or a stew in front of him.

Truth was, while he appreciated the motherly attentiveness, it was all getting to be a bit much.

But all that was soon to change.

On the third day, he was standing at the window looking out over the depressing vista when there was a knock on the door. He sighed despondently and muttered under his breath "At least she knocked this time" before calling, "one minute".

He hobbled back to the bed, struggling to breathe, and clutching his ribs, the pain from which seemed to get worse as the bones knitted together. He lay down and made himself comfortable. "Come in" he called.

The door opened and Ella, wearing the same pretty dress she was wearing when she first visited him in hospital, came in carrying a tray of food.

She shut the door and brought the tray to the bed. "Nell said I could see you if I made sure you ate this" she said.

"Another warder in the jailhouse" Ethan muttered his eyes rolling.

"And she said I had to plump your pillows".

"I think they've been plumped to within an inch of their life" Ethan said nodding towards the small table next to the bed. "Put the tray down over there, I'll eat it later".

Ella put down the tray down.

"Is this a social visit… or are you running an errand for that obnoxious good-for-nothing you're hooked up with?"

Ella's face dropped. She was hurt by that. "I'm sorry, I shouldn't have come" she said defensively before starting for the door.

"No, wait!" Ethan called after her.

She turned back barely looking at him.

"It's me that should be sorry. I shouldn't have said that. I've been cooped up in this room for three days going stir crazy and... Look, I'm sorry. Okay?"

Ella came back to the bed.

"Can we just start again?"

Ella nodded. "I just wanted to check you were on the mend, that's all".

"On the mend?" he frowned quizzically before the penny dropped. "Oh, I see. Getting better. Yes, I'm on the mend. Getting along just fine... apart from bursting at the seams from so much soup and stew. I'm sure my belly swelling is putting more pressure on my ribs".

Ella smiled, "Nell always did like to feed folks up. Her answer to everything". She hesitated, a little uncertain. "Anyway, I'd better go and let you get your rest. Just so long as you're okay".

"No, don't go, pull up a chair and stay a while" Ethan said nodding to a hard backed, wooden chair Nell had left there for when she came to check on him... which was far too often for Ethan's liking.

"Just for a minute, then I really have to go".

She pulled up the chair and sat down.

"You're not going to be in any trouble by being here, are you?" Ethan asked, adding when Ella didn't reply, "That man, Pyke. I get the feeling he might not be too pleased at you being here alone with me".

"I don't give a shit what Pyke thinks" Ella retorted. "Besides, we're hardly likely to be getting up to any funny business, are we?"

Ethan frowned quizzically.

"Not with you in that state"

Ethan smiled, seeing a forthrightness and spark of defiance in Ella he hadn't witnessed before.

"Yeah, I know" she said, "I can be a gobby cow sometimes. Think something and it's out'f my mouth before it has time to get to my brain. Gets me into trouble sometimes." She shrugged. "Most times, truth be told".

"A gal should always speak her mind".

Ella huffed ironically. "Yeah? Tell that to the women what live round here. What with my big gob and wearing my hair down, you'd think I was the spawn of the devil himself".

"Wearing your hair down?" Ethan questioned curiously.

"According to them only whores wear their hair down. Better that than piling your hair on top of your head like a cyst wrapped in bandages and ending up a shrivelled old biddy"

She looked around the room, anywhere but directly at Ethan. Played with her hands. More tentative and edgy than she was letting on.

"Why do you stay?" he asked. "Why don't you just get outta here? Start a new life"

"Where do you think I was going when Chalky Harris and his mates started grabbing my tits and slobbering all over me? Not that I'd have gone through with it, I don't suppose".

"Why not?"

"Spur of the moment thing when I found out…" she stopped herself from saying more with a shrug. "Nothing, it doesn't matter" she added.

There was an awkward silence and it was a while before she spoke again. When she did, there was a renewed sadness in her eyes.

"Anyway, even if I was to leave, where would I go and what would I do when I got there? Open my legs every time some bloke offered me a shilling? No thanks, I can do that here".

"At least you'd have decent air to breathe… and there must be choices other than whoring".

"Not for somebody like me, there's not"

"You could go back to school…"

"I'd have to have been there in the first place".

"You didn't go to school?"

"Sometimes. The rest of the time I'd be fetching and carrying for my dad".

She glanced at Ethan's Colt sitting next to the tray on the small table next to the bed. Changed the subject. "Is it true you can take a rabbits brain out through its arse without it even noticing?" she asked.

Ethan gave a laugh, clutching his ribs, "I think you might be getting me mixed up with Annie Oakley", he assured her.

Nell burst through the door in a fluster.

"You'd better go, your dad's downstairs looking for you, and if he finds you up here there'll be hell to pay" she blurted breathlessly.

Ella quickly sprang to her feet.

"I told him I hadn't seen you, but I don't think he believed me", Nell said, taking Ella's arm and ushering her towards the door. "Use the fire escape at the back".

There were heavy footsteps on the stairs. Ella froze, panic filling her eyes. Nell hurriedly closed the door.

"Quick, under the bed".

Ella scurried across the room, dropped to her knees, and slipped under the bed, only just hidden from sight before the door burst open and Nobby barged in with Frankie.

"Where is she?" Nobby barked.

"Hang on a minute" Nell replied, her casual sarcasm a match for his menacing scowl, "I'll take a look under the bed, shall I".

"Don't get smart with me, woman".

"That's difficult when the two of you don't have a brain cell between you. Open your eyes… she's not here".

Nobby's dark eyes searched the room.

Under the bed, Ella caught a whiff of the guzunder right next to her head and took a deep breath.

Nobby took one last look around.

"Satisfied?" Nell asked him.

"If I find you've been messing with me".

"You'll what? Give me a good hiding?"

Nobby fixed her with evil eyes.

Nell didn't shy away, stood her ground.

She marched across the room and held the door. "If that's all" she said unflinching.

"For now" Nobby replied.

"Good. Now piss off".

Nobby considered for a moment. "If you see her, tell her Pyke's looking for her. And he ain't happy".

Then he left, Frankie with him.

As Nell closed the door behind him and sighed with relief, Ella slipped out from under the bed and brushed down her dress.

"You'd better get out of here before he figures it out and comes back" Nell told her.

Ella continued to fiddle with her dress.

"Today, not tomorrow" she said, grabbing Ella's arm and dragging her to the door. "Now go!"

Ella looked back over her shoulder. At Ethan lying in the bed. "I'll come back later and..."

"Just go. Get outta here" Ethan told her.

Ella hurried out and Nell closed the door behind her. "I swear that girl will be the death of me one day" she said sighing despairingly before seeing the untouched tray on the table next to the bed.

"Here, you've been so wrapped up with talking to young Ella, you haven't touched your food" she insisted, grabbing the tray and placing it in Ethan's lap.

Ethan stared at the unappetising plate of food, turned up his nose and grimaced. "What the hell are those? The things that look like buffalo turds".

"Faggots".

"And they are exactly?"

"All the leftover bits of a pig wrapped up in its fatty stomach lining and then roasted".

"And the pile of mush sitting next to them?"

"Payse"

"What?"

"Peas" she enunciated. "Faggots and mushy payse with gravy, it's a delicacy round here".

"I'm sure it is" Ethan said unconvinced.

He pick up a fork and gingerly prodded one of the faggots with it. Moved it around the plate.

"I really am most grateful but…"

"Nonsense", Nell said, cutting in, "It's no trouble at all. Come on now, eat up".

Ethan tentatively cut off the edge of one of the faggots and, still grimacing, tasted it. He chewed it a couple of times and… Not bad. Not bad at all. Either that, or he was mightily hungry, and it didn't matter what it tasted like.

Nell fussed around. Tidying up. Picking up Ethan's clothes and sniffing them before tutting, "I need to get these in the washtub before they start walking about on their own". She tucked them under her arm.

"You and she close?" Ethan asked cutting another slice off the faggot.

"Somebody has to look out for her, and that father of hers isn't about to do it. Neither use nor ornament, that one".

"And her mother?"

"Died having her. I was there when she was born. I wrapped her up in blanket, handed her to Nobby and he just turned his back and walked off like she was a slab of meat gone off. The man doesn't have a feeling bone in his body".

Ethan contemplated for a moment, before taking a deep breath and sighing despairingly yet again. He seemed to be doing that a lot since he arrived in the Black Country. "How can you live like that? How can anybody live like that"?

"You either play the game with the cards you've been dealt, or cash in your chips and end it all. Choice's yours" she told him philosophically before bustling out with his washing.

Ethan shook his head in disbelief, he seemed to be doing a lot of that too. Took another bite of faggot.

CHAPTER 15

As Ella made her way across the dusty warehouse towards the stairs to Pyke's office, she went through her story in her mind. She had to get it straight, no mistakes, no faltering. One slip and Pyke would be on her like a ton of bricks. Then there would be a price to pay.

The obnoxious overlord was slouched slovenly in his chair when she came in as bright as she could muster. "Where the hell have you been?" he snarled menacingly.

"Down by the cut. It was nice day, so went for a walk" she replied casually.

"That's not what I heard" he said. "I heard you'd been seen sneaking into the pub".

"I wasn't sneaking anywhere" Ella protested. "I went to see Nell. No harm in that, is there?"

"So where were you when your dad came looking for you?" he asked accusingly.

Momentarily, Ella was caught off guard. She hesitated. "I... I don't know. I must have already left, I suppose. Anyway, why all the questions? What have I done wrong?"

"I don't know, you tell me" Pyke said, his eyes burning into her accusingly.

Ella just shrugged.

Pyke changed tack, "Anyway, forget all that" he said with a wave of his hand, "I've got a job for you. One you might like".

Ella's eyes narrowed suspiciously. First Pyke was telling her to forget something, and then the next minute offering her a job she might like. Pyke never forgot about anything, just stored it in the back of his devious mind to use against you when the time came. As for handing out titbits. He was most definitely up to something.

"That cowboy, the one that's convalescing down there".

"*Here it comes*", she thought to herself. "*Builds you up to knock you down*".

"Oh him" she said as casually as she could muster, "what about him?

"Now he's on the mend, I want you to go out'f your way to get to know him better".

That was the last thing Ella had been expecting. For a moment, she felt her heart flutter, then suspicion took over again. "Why the hell would I want to do that?" she asked trying her best to sound appalled at the idea.

"Because I told you to, that's why. I want you to keep an eye on him, make sure he don't start poking his nose in where it don't belong".

"He's hardly likely to go poking his nose anywhere, is he? Not stuck in bed all day" she replied far too quickly for Pyke's liking.

He tipped his head and his eyes narrowed, "How do you know he's stuck in bed all day?" he asked.

"When… when I went to the pub…

"Saw him, did you?"

"No I didn't see him" Ella bit indignantly. "Nell told me. Said it was a right pain in the arse having to be at his beck and call all day long".

"I bet it is" he said unconvinced.

"Anyway, what if I did see him? That's what you want, isn't it?"

"Aye, I do… but on my terms, not yours".

Ella stood there waiting.

"Well, what're you waiting for?" Pyke said fixing her with beady eyes.

Ella started to leave.

"Oh aye, and just you remember; when he's gone, I'll still be here. So when you're lying there with your legs open, you can curb your passion by remembering which side your bread's buttered. Now, piss off I've got work to do" he snapped with an air of finality.

Ella didn't want to appear too eager to carry out Pyke's instruction and stir up even more trouble for herself, so she left it a couple of days before visiting Ethan. By the time she got there, his breathing had gotten easier and he was already '*on the mend*'.

"I gotta get outta this place" he complained sulky as a kid who'd just had his candy confiscated. He swung his legs out of bed. "I swear, I'm gonna….".

"You're going to eat what Nell's prepared for you and stop complaining, that's what you're going to do" Ella chided him as she gently placed her hand on his shoulder to stop him getting up. "You can go out when Nell says you can. That was the agreement when Doc Harris agreed to you coming here".

Ethan flopped back on his pillow and sighed heavily. Ella picked up a tray from next to the bed and placed it in his lap.

"And the condemned man ate a hearty meal" Ethan mumbled miserably as he stared down at the food piled on a chipped white plate sitting on the tray.

Over the next few days, Ella visited regularly. She sauntered around the room reading to him from a book cradled in her hands, every now and then, pausing as he laughed out loud at something, she either said, or did, and they spent hours talking, about anything and everything. And as the days that went by, Ethan grew stronger. So much so, that by the end of the week he'd been granted parole from his prison cell above the bar.

Together, they had started to go out for walks, not caring who saw them, not Pyke, not the women who tutted and gossiped behind Ella's back calling her a slut and a slag. They were just two young people walking out together, enjoying one another's company and the freedom to wander wherever and whenever, they liked.

All this time Nell kept her counsel, even though, deep down, she was uneasy about the developing relationship that was clear for all to see. But something did not sit right with her. Something was wrong, she was sure of it. How could it be that Ella should be able visit Ethan so regularly without suffering any form of retribution from the slobbish puppet master who pulled the strings of almost every person in the town? It shouldn't be that easy. Never was. And if Pyke was allowing this fledgling relationship to blossom, then what was in it for him? He had to have a reason, and Pyke's reasons never bode well for anybody, no matter what his ulterior motive might be. But she continued to keep her counsel and didn't say anything, not a word, consoling herself in the fact that soon Ethan would be gone, and things would get back to normal; whatever normal might be. Besides, Ella was a young woman finding her feet after having spent her whole life living in hell, and hell would still be there waiting to greet her with open arms when this episode of her life was over, when her handsome young cowboy had long since returned to the open plains and clear blue skies of his homeland.

"*Make hay while the sun shines, sweetheart*" Nell thought to herself with an affectionate smile. "*Even if Pyke is the one cutting the bales*".

That didn't stop her worrying.

As the days went by, Ethan and Ella began to venture further and further afield, and one particular day found them strolling gently along the canal towpath.

Unusually for the time of the year, any time of the year in a land of eternal twilight, the sun had managed to claw its way through the clouds, and so it was warm and something approaching pleasant. In the distance, the castle surveyed all from atop of the hillside, and on either side of the murky soup that was the waterway, there were steep, overgrown, grassy banks. Every now and then the banks were broken by a stunted tree, it's bare, tentacle like branches casting long shadows as they hovered and swayed over the ash and crushed stone path.

For some time, an empty coal barge drawn by a heavy horse with a long, matted mane had been following them, its shod hooves clopping heavily on the hard pathway as it plodded steadily along. They stepped back and watched as the horse slowed to a stop short of the arched entrance to a narrow tunnel in the hillside, its mouth reflected in the water to form a perfect circle. A porthole to some bleak and uninviting world.

The barge drifted into the pathway and one of the two bargees, his face and shapeless, ill-fitting clothes sooty with coal dust, placed his foot on the edge of the barge and jumped ashore. He raised his fingers to his mouth and whistled before starting to untie the tow line from the horse. A scruffy, grubby faced kid no more than ten or eleven years old, his long-sleeved shirt rolled up to his elbows and only half tucked into his shorts, appeared out of nowhere, running at full tilt over the brow of the bank and down the steep slope at the side of the tunnel entrance. The bargee tossed him a penny. The kid bit on it and shoved it in his pocket before taking the horse's bridle. Only then did lead the horse away, up the track and over the brow.

The bargee climbed aboard again. He picked up a large pole and was about to shove off when...

"Hey, mister" Ella called to him.

The bargee looked over.

Ella glanced at Ethan, smiling impishly as he raised his eyebrows and furrowed his brow. Then she skipped over to the barge and for a few moments she and the bargee engaged in muted conversation. The bargee looked over at the cowboy, grinning as he turned back to Ella and nodded his head.

Ella waved for Ethan to join them.

"What's going on?" Ethan asked apprehensively as he approached them.

"You'll see" Ella replied obscurely, having already taken the hand offered to her by the bargee.

She put her foot on the side of the barge and hopped aboard. Sat down on the clean blanket the second bargee had taken from a lidded box and thrown over the thick layer of black soot covering the bench at the back of the barge.

Ethan continued to hesitate.

"Not afeared are you? A big mon like you" the first bargee scoffed chortling.

Ethan took the hand held out to him and gingerly climbed aboard. And as he sat down next to Ella, she turned to him, tossed her head back and laughed. The colour had totally drained from his face.

The bargee shoved off with the pole and the barge started to slowly drift across the water towards the tunnel entrance. Ethan, not knowing what to expect, what it was that awaited them in the darkness, gripped the edge of the bench, his knuckles turning as white as his ashen face. Imagine his surprise when the two bargees dropped down two hard wooden boards and lay on them, flat on their backs. Ethan glanced at Ella with a quizzical frown, looking for reassurance. Ella simply smiled, took his hand, and squeezed it reassuringly.

And they drifted into the netherworld.

The darkness was all-consuming and the deathly, eerily silent, the silence broken only by the splashing of the barge passing through the putrid water and the strained inhalations of the bargees' heavy breathing.

There was the sharp scratch of a match being struck and a moment later the blackness was broken by the flickering, dancing glow of torchlight that sparkled in Ella's eyes and reflected on the walls of an oppressive passageway no more than five feet high and just over seven feet wide that was chiselled through the hillside below Dudley castle. The bargees would usually make their journey through this unearthly cocoon in total darkness, but that was when they weren't carrying passengers, folks who got spooked by the dark and feared they had already died and were being transported to their final, lonely resting place.

A chill wind passing through the tunnel brushed across Ethan's face raising the hairs on his neck and sending shivers down his spine. He was one of those people. Like them, he didn't like the dark, never had done, not since he had once found himself trapped in a collapsed mineshaft and sat there alone for twelve long, desperate hours waiting for his rescuers to arrive, never knowing if he would escape the oppressive mausoleum dead or alive.

Ethan distracted himself from the nightmare by watching the bargees 'leg it'. It was a sight he had never seen before and, as fascinating as it was, one he hoped he would never see again. Lying flat on their backs, the two men walked on the walls of the tunnel, their gruelling efforts propelling the barge slowly and silently along the narrow artery.

For Ethan, the journey couldn't end soon enough. It seemed to last an eternity. Then, just when he felt he couldn't suffer any more, thankfully the heavy, strained breathing of the bargees grew shallower and louder as they made one last effort, pushing towards a pinpoint of light in the distance, a light that shone like a beacon of hope in a place where previously there had been none.

At first, the curtain of vines that guarded egress to the tunnel was barely discernible. But then, as the barge approached and finally passed through them, they draped verdant green with small white flower buds all around the barge, embracing them like a mother's welcoming arms.

As the barge emerged from the tunnel and into the basin beyond, Ethan's eyes widened, and he gasped with incredulity. It was as mystical as it was magical, an oasis of breath-taking beauty and colour in a world full of gloom and wretchedness. All around, flowering bushes dotted the steep banks as they swept high above to form a circle of blue, an eye to the heavens through which insects and bees flitted in enchanted, fairylike beams of sunlight that shone through it and down onto the rippling water below. Not that the water was any clearer.

The barge pulled over and dropped Ella and Ethan off on a narrow bank of loose shale. They waved the men off again, watching and waiting until the bargees had once more dropped to their backs and the barge had passed through yet another a curtain of vines into a second darkened tunnel entrance on the other side of the basin.

Ella led Ethan up the bank towards the window of blue. All around them, the ground was strewn with foliage, small, leafy green trees and bushes and plants, some of them bearing colourful buds and flowers in bloom. Ella had no idea what their names were, or even what species they were. All she knew was, that they were pretty, prettier than anything she could ever remember seeing anywhere else in the world in which she lived.

Halfway up the bank, Ella flopped to the ground and Ethan sat down beside her, neither speaking at they sat in the peaceful silence and solitude of the basin.

Ethan looked up as a flock of birds flew across the sky above. "It's beautiful here" he said quietly.

"I used to come here with my brother, Tommy" Ella said with a distant look in her eye.

Ethan looked questioningly.

"We were twins" Ella told him before continuing. "Every Sunday morning would get up early, scrub our faces, dress up in our best for chapel, and afterwards we'd come up here. It was our secret place".

Momentarily, she paused and reflected in silence. Then she said sadly, "That was before the fever got him".

"The fever".

"That's what you get from drinking the water round here. Most of its stagnant and contaminated by all the shit it has pumped into it, that's why most folks die before they get to a ripe old age. It's better if you work in the mines, mind".

Ethan's raised a brow and his eyes narrowed, "You live longer if you work in the mines? Doesn't make sense".

"Course it does" she corrected him like it was obvious, "if you work underground you don't drink the water, do you? You take your snap and ale to swill it down with. Ale's been processed before you drink it so…"

She shrugged.

Ethan waited a moment before asking, "What happened to him?" although he felt he already knew the answer.

"He died" she replied quite matter of fact.

"How old was he?"

"Just turned eleven". She paused a moment remembering him. "At the funeral Reverend Price spouted his comforting words and afterwards folks cried and said how sorry they were. Me? I just smiled, glad that he got out before the place had time to drag him down like it does the rest of us".

For a while, they sat bathing in the silence and tranquillity, and watched as yet another barge, one loaded with coal this time, emerged through the verdant curtain on one side, and crossed the basin before disappearing into the tunnel mouth on the other.

"What's it like? The place you come from" Ella asked once the barge had disappeared.

"Nothing like here, that's for sure," Ethan replied with a quiet huff, "There's wide open, grassy plains that stretch as far as the eye can see. Sunlight sparkles and dances in crystal clear streams flowing down from the mountains, the water so clear you can see right down to the stones laying in the bottom.

He paused a moment, reflecting dreamily.

Ella hung on every word.

"Not a stone's throw away, there's a river that's so wide you can barely see to the other side. When I was a kid, we would go swimming there. We would race down after school was done for the day, strip off our clothes, dive into the water and be instantly invigorated. And when we were done foolin' around, we would spread out on the banks alongside to dry off, just lay there naked gazing up at the clear blue sky with fluffy white clouds drifting across it".

"Sounds like paradise"

"It is, Close, anyways".

Ella thought for a moment. Then she said, "We used to swim in here when I came up with Tommy".

Ethan looked down at the murky waters you couldn't even see through, turned up his nose and grimaced in disgust. Then back to Ella, "You used to swim here? Was it safe?"

"Course it was safe. There's no barges on a Sunday" Ella replied like it was a daft question.

"I was thinking more of the state of the water. It hardly looks hygienic", Ethan assured her.

Ella shrugged, like that's just the way it is. "You always lived out there in the west, have you? In paradise? she mocked with a smile.

Ethan laughed and then fell quiet again.

"The Colonel took me in when I was just six years old. My folks had been killed in a railroad accident. He's like a father to me. Taught me to fish, hunt, ride... and how to fight back when I got bullied in the schoolyard.

"You bullied?" Ella huffed, "I can't imagine that"

"Believe it or not, when I was young, I was scrawny as one of those sparrows I've seen flying around town, nervous too. What is it you folks say over here... 'wouldn't say shoo to a chicken?"

"Goose" Ella laughed. "Wouldn't say boo to a goose".

Ethan shrugged, "Wouldn't say boo to a goose"

They fell into yet another peaceful silence. Then, after a couple of minutes, Ella suddenly jumped to her feet. "Right, time to go" she insisted brightly.

Ethan's face darkened. "We have to brave that tunnel again?" he asked fearfully.

"Not this time. We can walk" Ella said starting up the steep bank. "It's not far".

Thankful for small mercies, Ethan got to his feet and followed her to the top, trudging after her over the uneven ground. And when they reached the rim of the basin, when they reached the top of the hillside, there spread out in front of them not a stone's throw away, was the town in all its lack of glory. But most surprising of all, it was surrounded by open countryside, rolling hills, green fields and a small woodland sitting on top of a hill, the town with its smoking towers and burning flames, an obscene, nauseating blot tarnishing the heart of the English countryside its writers so poetically refer to as '*England's green and pleasant land*'.

"And you made me suffer that journey through the tunnel when we could've just walked here?" Ethan said with wide eyed incredulity and disbelief.

"Cissy" Ella said with a laugh.

Ethan knitted his brow and narrowed his eyes "Cissy?" he repeated not knowing what the hell one of those was. Then he shook his head and followed Ella as she skipped down towards the town.

CHAPTER 16

For the deeply religious people of the Black Country, Monday to Saturday was for working and Sunday was devoted to the Lord. It was a day when you gave thanks for everything gifted you in life, and fell to your knees and prayed for the strength that, come Monday morning, in spite of everything this harsh place had to throw at you, you would still be there waiting patiently for the whole sorry, soul destroying process to start all over again.

Sunday was also a day of rest and recuperation when, for twenty-four hours at least, factory doors were closed, foundry hammers fell silent, furnaces were extinguished and there were no choking smoke clouds to billow from the monolithic chimney stacks and further pollute the toxic air that folks were forced to breath for the rest of the week. Apart from the chores of the womenfolk who, dressed in their threadbare pinnies wrapped over dowdy, ill-fitting dresses, would painstakingly prepare the victuals that would sustain the family for the rest of the week. There was nothing that should be done on a Sunday that couldn't wait until Monday. It was a way of life, a constant drummed into them from the very first day they started at Sunday school in the dusty box room behind the Methodist chapel, and right there at the heart of the strident sermons delivered with such gusto and vitriol by the passionate Reverend Price, who peddled his beliefs from the pulpit when they were older.

"It's right there in the good book" he would insist vehemently. "And on the seventh day God rested. It is God's law, and who are we to flagrantly disobey the commands of our Lord Almighty?"

God's law it might be, but not on that particular Sunday morning, on that particular Sunday morning God's wrath and requiting punishment for their flagrant delinquency was the last thing on the minds of the people of the Black Country.

Buoyed by memories of Buffalo Bill's wild west show just a few weeks earlier, as they gathered in small cliques outside the chapel after morning service, the townsfolk bedecked in their Sunday best, the womenfolk dressed all in black and wearing hats instead of turbans, and the men with the top button of their collarless shirts fastened and with their hair greased back neatly, were buzzing. It was a big day. The day when the travelling picture show came to town... and this time it carried with it a real treat.

127

Earlier in the year, '*The Great Train Robbery*', a silent film made by a man named Edward S. Porter for the Edison Manufacturing Company, had been released in America and was an instant commercial success. It was a western and although it wasn't freely available in England at the time, the owner of the picture show, '*Lucky Joe*' Carter, had, by devious means known only to himself, managed to get his hands on a copy and was now peddling it around the country... and making money hand over fist in the process.

Later that evening, an eager queue began to form outside the Methodist Hall at the rear of the chapel. Men, women and children, the girls in pretty dresses and white ankle socks, the boys for once scrubbed clean and with their hair brushed. Parked up alongside the hall, there was a closed carriage on the side of which was painted in gaudy, scrolling letters, "*Lucky Joe Carter's Travelling Picture Show*". A tethered horse was munching happily on a fresh bale of hay close by. The steady hum of excitement and anticipation was palpable.

At first Reverend Price, a slightly overweight man with what might be regarded as a beer belly had he not been stridently tea total - drinking, another of God's dictates that was quietly pushed to one side by the majority of working men who spent most of the hours between work and sleep in the pub - had baulked at the idea of purveying such wanton blasphemy on a Sunday. But that was before he had encountered the strength of feeling amongst his congregation who, or so it would seem, were not so God fearing as he thought they should be when it came to their entertainment.

"If God hadn't intended us to see the show, then why would he send Joe Carter?" they had argued with conviction. "It's God's sign".

Reverend Price was vociferous in his defence, "Joe Carter has not been sent here by the Good Lord, he is the physical embodiment of the devil himself come here for one purpose and one purpose alone, to place temptation in the face of the righteous".

"Is that the same devil what pours your port every Christmas while we get a bollocking for having a pint after work, is it?" one of the men asked bitterly.

"That's different" the Reverend had protested defensively, trotting out the old chestnut. "That's for medicinal purposes only".

"Cures your gout, no doubt" the man had replied, which promoted sardonic laughter from the folks accompanying him. "And I wonder how you got that?"

Realising he had been pushed into a corner, Reverend Price had squirmed for a few minutes before finally relenting and granting his permission. But he still wasn't happy about it. He wasn't happy at all, and as they waited in line before making their way inside, he stood at the hall door observing the blasphemous carryings on with a face that was a dark as any canal tunnel.

In his seedy lair high above the warehouse, slouched in his chair, Jacko at his side, Pyke had assembled his gang of hardened thugs and criminals and was issuing his

129

instructions to the men standing in a semi-circle facing him. Billy, Tommy, Abel, a man named Frankie and the man with the wide scar running across his cheek, Chalky Harris. Chalky seemed nervous and edgy, like he was half expecting news of his earlier indiscretion under the canal bridge to have filtered back to Pyke and he would now be facing undoubtedly painful repercussions. But they never came. Either Pyke didn't know, or perhaps he had something else in mind.

"It needs to be quick and fast" Pyke slobbered unequivocally. "You need to get in there quick as you can and out again before anybody latches on to what's happening. Has the chance to sound the alarm. Any slip ups and we're bollocksed".

Chalky breathed a sigh of relief.

Heads nodded all around.

"Good!".

He jabbed his pudgy finger at Frankie standing on the end. "You wait by the track with the cart and keep an eye out for anybody looking to poke their nose in where it don't belong. There's a pot of gold waiting at the end of this if we pull it off right, so don't fuck it up".

He waved them away and they started for the door.

Pyke put his hand to his head, frustration getting the better of him, "Oh, for fuck's sake".

The men turned back.

"Aren't you forgetting something?"

The men looked at one another. Confused.

Pyke put his index finger to his temple and squeezed it. "Bang" he said, exhaling and rolling his eyes

The penny dropped.

"Oh, ah" Billy said going to a box in the corner and opening it up. The others followed suit. And as they took arms from the box, handguns and rifles, Pyke barked instructions. "Just remember" he insisted, "they're for show only so don't go wavin' 'em around all over the place getting somebody hurt. Not his time".

"Goin' soft in your old age, are you Pykie?" Billy said without thinking, instantly realising he should have kept his mouth firmly shut. "Just jokin' Pykie, I didn't mean anything by it. Honest" he added quickly.

"You'd better be" Pyke warned him menacingly.

Billy half-smiled and went back to the job in hand.

"Right, now bugger off the lot of you... and if you fuck it up, don't bother coming back unless you're willing to suffer the consequences".

After they had all left, Pyke turned to Jacko by his side. "When this is over, I want him to suffer, I don't like smart arses. Oh aye, and that other matter we were talking about... take care of that, an' all while you're at it".

Jacko nodded his subservience.

Amongst those waiting to gain entrance to the hall were Ella and Ethan. Ethan waited patiently and Ella bubbled excitedly along with everybody else, ignoring the sly sideways glances of the men who looked her up and down lasciviously and the scornful glares of the straight-laced women who accompanied them. Mostly, that is. Until one of the women tutted and shook her head with disgust.

131

Ella bobbed her tongue out her.

The woman's lips thinned, and her eyes narrowed, her eyebrows running into one.

"Do you have to do that?" Ethan objected awkwardly, clearly embarrassed.

If Ella felt herself chastised, she did a good impression of hiding it. "Bitter old cow" she huffed haughtily. "I bet she hasn't had her knicker elastic twanged this side of Christmas".

Ethan was saved from any further embarrassment when the doors opened and 'Lucky Joe' Carter, a short, chubby man dressed in a brown and light grey chequered suit, a multi-coloured dickie bow clipped to his starched high-collar shirt and with a black bowler on his head that dropped down to all but cover his eyes, stepped out of the hall.

"Your attention please, ladies and gentlemen".

The eager crowd continued to chatter.

"Attention please" Joe insisted loudly, like a schoolmaster calling assembly to order. He clapped his hands and the chattering finally stopped. All eyes turning to him as he commenced his overly verbose patter.

"Felicitations, fine ladies and upstanding gentlemen. Through these doors there lies, for your utmost delight and delectation, a wonderous theatre of luminosity, a world of magic and wonder, a captivating playhouse where you will be treated to a cornucopia of delights that will bombard your senses and set your head spinning".

He paused for effect.

The townsfolk hung onto his every word.

"Tonight, ladies and gents, I cordially invite you join me there, to accompany me on a spine-tingling adventure that is as mesmerising as it is breath-taking, to journey with me to a place where you will be mesmerised and transfixed, perfectly engrossed, titillated to a point of divine ecstasy as you are transported to a place that is as barren as it is resplendent, as wild as it is magnificent, a tempestuous and untamed land where history was made and legend was conceived. Ladies and gentlemen, I humbly bring to you...

He paused and the townsfolk held their breath. He stepped to one side, took off his hat and with an almost regal bow and a low, flourishing wave of his hand, he bade folks to join him in his palace of light.

"... the American Wild West".

Reverend Price tutted, thoroughly disapproving, and watched with disgust as the chatter started all over again and folks started to file into the hall.

Ethan couldn't believe the theatrics of it all... and that was coming from a man who spent his whole life travelling the world with Buffalo Bill.

"Tickets please" Joe requested taking their tickets at the door. "Thank you... Thank you very much... Go right it". He rubbed the hair of a young kid who stared up at him wide eyed. "Enjoy the show" he told him with a wink.

The inside of the hall had been laid out with rows of chairs and an aisle between them, in front of which were two long kneelers borrowed, much to the disgust of the

Reverend, from the chapel to accommodate all those extra people who had bought tickets. Ella came in with Ethan, and once they had taken their seats, she looked around barely able to contain her excitement. At the front of the room, positioned so that everyone was afforded a clear view of it, there was a large, grubby white screen that looked that it might once have been someone's bedsheet, and on the walls, there were posters advertising the show and forthcoming attractions. At the back of the room, a film projector rested on a high set of wooden steps. On the far side, tucked away in the corner, there was a battered organ brought in specially for the occasion.

"Oh, my God, just look at her, will you?" Ella suddenly blurted.

Sitting at the organ was Joe's wife, Jessie. A counterpoint to her husband, where Joe was short and rotund, Jessie was a stick thin, a hawkish faced woman who surveyed the audience like she was a bird of prey searching greedily for its next meal.

"She's got a face like a slapped arse".

The woman seated in front of her tutted her disgust and her husband sitting next to her supressed a smile. Ethan simply rolled his eyes. He seemed to be doing that a lot since he came to the Black Country.

Carter was just closing the outside door when Pyke waddled up, Jacko at his side. "Good evening, gentlemen" he said welcoming them warmly. "Tickets, please".

"We don't have none" Pyke assured him without missing a stride as he continued to make his way inside.

"In that case, I am afraid entry is not permitted on this fine evening. Only those with tickets may attend this evening's performance".

Pyke stopped and stared at him hard. "You sure about that, are you?" he asked eying the man through beady eyes "If you are, I'd think about reconsidering".

Carter had a yellow streak that ran right the way down his spine, and although he was overbearing and irritating, he was not stupid; he knew instantly when he was being threatened.

He forced a smile as he stepped aside.

A hush fell as Pyke came in with Jacko and made his way along the aisle. Ethan watched as, part way down, he stopped and stared darkly at Ella. Clearly uncomfortable, she turned away from him and Pyke continued on his way towards the front.

"What was that all about?" Ethan asked.

Ella shook her head. Bit her lip.

Pyke stood over a man in the front row. Clearly feeling threatened, the man immediately got up and stepped to one side. Pyke stared at the man's wife who had been sitting beside him. "You an' all" he said bobbing his head towards the back of the room.

The woman stood up. Her husband took her arm and guided her towards the back of the room. Pyke sat down, Jacko next to him.

Still looking ashen from his encounter with Pyke, Carter came in and closed the door behind him. He nodded at Reverend Price standing to one side observing proceeding. Clearly put out at being ordered around in his own sacred domain, the minister pouted his disapproval but put the lights out, nonetheless.

Particles of dust danced like fairy dust in a beam of light from the projector that shone over the heads of the audience. Scratches and scrapes flitted on the soiled screen and, as the film's title shakily appeared there, Jessie started to play the addled organ music that was to accompany it.

Then, and only then, the film began.

Silent apart from Jessie's organ playing, the film's narrative unfolded in silent, over exposed, jerky movements. The action opened in a telegraph office in America's Wild West, where a conscientious clerk representing the railroad company was blissfully unaware of the imminent danger he was in as he quietly beavered away doing his company duty. Without warning, the door burst open and two masked bandits rushed in, holding him at gunpoint as they ordered him to have a train stopped at a trackside water tank, allaying any suspicion that anything untoward might be happening, by telling the driver that the water in the locomotive's tender was running low and needed replenishing. Fearing for his life, the terrified clerk did exactly as he was told and fired off the message, receiving a heavy blow to the back of his head as a reward. Not wasting any time, the bandits then bound him hand and foot, and scarpered tout de suite leaving him unconscious on the floor.

Connecting rods attached to the wheels of a steam locomotive pumped relentlessly as they drove the heavy wheels of the train trailing several closed carriages. Through the windows of the cab up front, lights illuminated the way ahead, shining down onto the track and spilling over and up onto the steep, overgrown banks dotted with trees rising on either side. In the distance, the lights fell onto a wooden cart across the track next to a station box, the horse that pulled it still hitched. The train driver pulled on the chain hanging just over his head. The whistle atop the boiler that pumped clouds of steam into the air sounded a shrill warning, the connecting rods slowed, and the wheels screeched as they came to a full stop just short of the cart.

"You'd better take a look" the train's driver said to the engineer who, bathed in glistening sweat, had broken off from stoking the blood red fiery furnace with coal.

The engineer gave him a sideways glance before backing up, stepping out onto the ladder, and climbing down from the cab onto the side of the track.

Jessie's organ playing grew more and more intense, the audience enthralled as, on the constantly flickering makeshift screen, the train came to a full stop alongside the water tower and the two bandits appeared with two more of their band of hard-hearted marauders. They quickly climbed aboard the train, two of them heading straight to the express car, two to the cab where…

The train driver's eyes widened in terror as he found a gun barrel pressing against his temple. "Don't do anything silly and we can all get out'f this unscathed" Tommy, a scarf covering his nose and mouth so that he was unrecognisable, warned him with quiet menace.

The driver swallowed hard and nodded.

"You'd better go and see what he's up to" Tommy said with one eye on the engineer who was only just visible in the gloom further along the track. Chalky nodded subserviently.

Abel and Billy, burst into one of the carriages further back, surprised to find a guard dozing as he rested against the side of a large wooden crate with a rifle propped in his lap. Startled by the din the guard immediately woke, grabbed his firearm, leapt to his feet and…

Billy shot him in the head in cold blood, blood and brains splattering against the side of the carriage and over the crate.

"What the fuck did you do that for?" Abel demanded to know.

"He was goin' for you, Abel" Billy insisted. "Would've killed you an' all if I hadn't stopped him".

The theatre audience remained enthralled.

Having forced the engineer to disconnect the locomotive from the rest of the train, the bandits usher the passengers from the carriages at gunpoint and frisk them down, relieving them of anything and everything they thought might be valuable.

A violent explosion blew open the door of a safe at the back of the carriage and, as the smoke began to clear, Billy and Abel hurriedly scooped the cash and papers secreted inside it into the hessian bags they had been carrying with them.

In the locomotive at the front of the train, Tommy and Chalky hastily bound the driver and engineer hand and foot, back to back, before stuffing rag in their mouths to stop them from raising the alarm.

In the telegraph office, the bound operator was still out cold when his daughter came in bringing him a meal on a tray. Rapidly, she cut him free from the ropes binding him and brought him around by dousing him with water. He immediately jumped to his feet and rushed out.

The audience crowded in the Methodist Hall laughed out loud as, up on the screen, customers in a dance hall fired shots at the feet of a tenderfoot who had wandered in unsuspecting, the man panicking as he danced, hopping comically from foot to foot.

The door slammed open and the telegraph operator rushed in, hastily telling them what had happened. They quickly formed a posse to chase the bandits down.

The doors to the carriage slid open to reveal Abel and Billy standing there. Frankie, driving the cart, pulled up alongside. Almost before it had stopped, Billy and Abel were sliding the crate out of the carriage and onto the back of the cart where Tommy was waiting to make sure it was resting safe before securing it with rope.

In the Methodist Hall where the audience sat on the edge of the seats mesmerised as they held their breath, Jessie's addled organ music became more and more frantic as it accompanied the pictures on screen.

The crate secure, Billy and Abel tossed the hessian sacks down to Tommy where he stowed them safely. Then they jumped over themselves leaving the carriage door wide open. Tommy shouted to Frankie "Right, let's go". Frankie slapped the horse's reins and a moment later the cart was trundling up a broken path between the trees growing at the side of the signal box, off and away into the night.

Jessie's addled organ music continued to rise, reaching fever pitch as the posse, the hooves of their horses kicking up clouds of sandy dust, chased the bandits at full tilt through the mountains. Eventually they caught up with them and, in a blaze of gunfire, smoke puffing from the barrels of their pistols, the bandits were overcome, and the mail, documents and other valuables stolen from the train were recovered.

The leader of the outlaws emptied his pistol right down lens of the camera. Just why he would want to do that was anybody's guess, the question remaining unanswered, as was the question of how he managed to do it anyway when he had just been captured. Not that it mattered, nobody gave two hoots about it making sense.

The audience were on their feet in a shot, clapping and cheering wildly as the credits were shown. Jessie's accompaniment began to fade, and the screen flickered and flashed, before eventually the hall fell into darkness.

At the back of the room, Joe glanced across at the Reverend Price still standing next to the door, hoping he would turn on the lights. But the venerated preacher didn't even notice him, his rapturous applause more animated and enthusiastic than anybody.

As the crowd filed out of the hall, they chattered excitedly, their offspring dodging behind the closed carriage, phutting and firing off make believe gunshots. For many of them, next to the visit of Buffalo Bill it had most probably been the greatest night of their miserable lives. A night they would never forget.

Ethan smiled as Ella bubbled along beside him. "It's nothing like that, you know. Not really".

But Ella wasn't listening, her eyes transfixed as she stared behind him. Ethan looked back over his shoulder to see Pyke, his lapdog Jacko inevitably at his side, standing in the shadow at the side of the hall and fixing them with cold beady eyes.

"Out west, a stone would mark that man's resting place on Boot Hill". Ethan said taking Ella's arm. "Come on, let's get outta here.

Ella let Ethan lead her out onto the street, but not without one last furtive look back over her shoulder.

CHAPTER17

"Why are we up here?" Ethan asked as Ella led him up a darkened side street towards the castle.

"You'll see" she replied with a mischievous hint of mystery in her eyes.

At the top of the street, a black iron gate barred their way. Ella rattled the heavy padlock locked in place by an even heavier chain. "Help me up" she said.

With a look of uncertainty, Ethan cupped his hands in front of him, Ella stepped into them… and in a flash was up and over.

Minutes later, they were walking through the castle grounds as they made their way towards the derelict remains of what had once been a wooden motte and bailey castle built around the time of the Norman invasion. Not that that was what loomed over them right then. The motte and bailey castle had been replaced a millennium earlier by a stone fortification that, in the intervening years, had itself been demolished and replaced numerous times.

What remained was but a shell of the defensive stronghold it once was.

They passed through a tall, arched stone gateway that once would have been barred to unwelcome visitors by a stout wooden gate, and into a wide courtyard surrounded by a broken-down curtain wall and what remained of living quarters once bustling with activity.

On the far side of the courtyard, they came to an open doorway in a looming tower and Ella disappeared into the darkness within without missing a stride.

Moments later, her head reappeared. "Come on, you'll be fine" she encouraged Ethan who had hesitated apprehensively. Then she disappeared again.

'*Man up cissy is what she means*" Ethan thought to himself as he stood nervous, before swallowing hard, bracing himself and stepping into the dimly lit stairwell.

As Ethan made his way up the narrow, spiral staircase, carefully picking his way on stone steps worn smooth by the centuries, he could barely see his hand in front of his face, and the walls were so close they felt like they were about to fall in on him. Apart from the echo of Ella's footsteps from above as she skipped up the steps like a mountain goat, it was deathly silent.

Part way up, he paused for a moment, not so much because he needed a breather, but because he needed to compose himself. And as he stood there, suddenly, Ella's footsteps stopped and there was nothing left but an eerie silence that sent a shiver down his spine.

"Alright, I'm coming" he muttered to himself before continuing his journey to the top. "Though how I get down again? That's another question".

None too soon, Ethan emerged from the stairwell and onto the narrow battlements that ran around the top of the tower, his already ashen face instantly fell when he saw Ella crouched on the floor, leaning against the wall, her knees up under her chin as she wrapped her arms around them and swayed back and forth.

Ella was quietly groaning as he rushed to her side and dropped to his haunches next to her. "What is it? What's wrong?" he asked helplessly as he placed a reassuring hand on her shoulder.

"Nothing. It's nothing".

"It doesn't look like…"

"I've got the rags on, - alright?" she snapped sharply. "Now, are you happy?"

"The rags on?" Ethan frowned.

"A woman's curse. Now, bugger off and leave me be" she yelled shrugging his hand off her shoulder.

Ethan hesitated a moment before standing up and making his way to the other end of the protective parapet that looked out over the town. And as he looked out, he wondered if, many centuries earlier, some medieval knight had stood in that self-same spot, loading his bow, and firing arrows through the crenels before dodging behind the merlons for protection from the missiles projected from below. It was a fanciful thought and one as far removed from the fighting that took place in the old west as he could possibly imagine.

After a while, Ella appeared at his side as though nothing had happened. "What time is it?".

Ethan took a watch from his pocket and looked at it, barely able to make out the hands in the dim, moonless light. "Five minutes to midnight" he said returning the watch to his pocket.

"It won't be long now"

"For what?" Ethan asked as he gazed out over the grey buildings that filled the skyline.

"You'll see".

Ethan continued to stare at the skyline. "There's been something I've been wanting to tell you all night" he said quietly, "I just didn't know how".

"I know"

"You do?"

"You're leaving. Nell told me. When?"

"In the morning. The train departs at eight sharp" he hesitated momentarily. "Meeting you is the only thing that has made this whole experience bearable and... it would mean a lot if you could be there to see me off".

A low, rising rumble broke the strained silence and you could feel the ground shake. "Here it comes now".

Ethan gasped out loud as a burning lance of flame speared into the dull, overcast night sky, like a fearsome, angry dragon spewing its fiery breath devouring everything in its path. A moment later a second lance of flame belched from one of the many phallic chimney stacks dotting the horizon. Then another. Another. And another until, in the blink of an eye, the whole of the skyline was aflame. It was as though the earth had cracked

145

open and the bowels of hell were spilling out in violent retribution.

Ethan look up in awe. High above him the swirling clouds were etched with every colour imaginable. Deep, vibrant hues of red and orange and yellow and... it was magical, mesmerising, just like Ethan imagined the celestial ballet of the Northern Lights to be. But this wasn't an aurora of pirouetting light gifted in its magnificence by Mother Nature herself, this was very much a man-made spectacle. A necessary evil.

It was one minute past midnight on Monday morning and the working week had just begun.

Just before eight o'clock the following morning Ethan, instantly recognisable in his wide-brimmed hat and long white Slicker, made his way through the ornate arched entrance to the railway station and out onto the platform where the morning train awaited its departure. He placed his saddlebag down on the ground at his feet and took a look around. It was quiet, just a handful of people escaping the squalor as they journeyed for work in nearby towns and cities, although just why anyone of them would choose to live there in the first place was an unfathomable mystery to him.

He looked around, watching, and waiting, waiting for her to come and say goodbye before he left. He was still waiting when the station porter approached him just before eight.

"If you're travelling, mister, you'd best get on board", the man in the dark blue uniform and peaked cap informed him with a distinct lack of formality, "it'll be leaving in two minutes".

Ethan took one last look around, picked his saddlebag, slung it over his shoulder, crossed the platform and stepped into the waiting carriage.

Ethan placed his saddlebag on the overhead storage rack, took off his hat, tossed in onto the seat opposite and sat down, craning forward to stare out of the window in case she came late, and he missed her. She didn't.

From outside he heard a voice call "All aboard" followed by several doors slamming. The whistle sitting atop the locomotive at the front of the train sounded twice. This was immediately followed by the gushing whoosh of steam being released, and a moment later the station was obscured in a drifting cloud of thick, grey, damp mist.

Ethan sagged back in his seat. The mist began to slowly dissipate. And as it did so, a barely discernible, almost ethereal figure began to appear at its heart. Ethan's pulse quickened as he craned forward to get a better look. The cloud slowly thinned, drifted away and...

Standing on the platform staring in at him was Hindbuck, his hands in the pockets of his long, dark greatcoat and with his bowler on his head.

Ethan raised his hand and shielded his face and kept his head down, hoping beyond hope that Hindbuck would just walk on by as he ambled down the aisle towards him. He didn't. As he reached the place where Ethan was sitting, he stopped and looked down.

147

Ethan looked up and frowned quizzically, his face filled with confusion.

"Sorry, Mister Baker, I'm afraid I'm going to have to ask you to come with me" Hindbuck said leaving no room for argument.

CHAPTER 18

Ethan walked at Hindbuck's side as they ambled along the towpath heading towards a stone bridge over the canal just outside town. It was just as though they were two colonial gentlemen out for a leisurely afternoon stroll... other than the fact that Ethan was seething and his was blood boiling.

"What the hell's is this?" he demanded.

"All in good time, Mister Baker" the policeman replied casually.

Ethan looked away and gritted his teeth, clenched his fists as Hindbuck began to ramble on irritatingly.

"You wouldn't believe it, but there was a time when this whole area was cut off from the world, nothing coming in or going out unless it was delivered by horse and cart over land. So the folks had to rely on making small things for a living, nails, chains, locks, and hinges. That sort of thing. Then, somebody came up with the bright idea of navigating a canal through the hillside and all that changed. Before you could say Jack Robinson, they were digging out coal and iron from under the hill and shipping it out all over the place. Course, when the train came along, everything changed yet again".

He paused for a moment, reflecting with a hint of sadness. "All that and the so-called industrial revolution made us what we are today. God help us".

Ethan had reached the end of his tether, he hadn't asked for a history lesson. "Are you going to tell me what the hell's going on any time soon?" he snapped angrily.

"Like I said, Mister Baker. All in good time".

And the time came soon. Without missing a stride, out of the blue Hindbuck suddenly said, "Ah there it is now".

"What is?"

"The crime scene" Hindbuck replied striding forward.

Ethan looked, curious to see what all the fuss was about. Up ahead, just short of the bridge, Penny was taking a statement from two bargees standing next to a coal barge moored alongside the towpath. On the other side of the path, a second uniformed police officer was bending down next to something lying in the grass on the bank.

"Are these the two men who found the body" Hindbuck asked as he approached Penny.

"Yes, sir. I was just taking a statement".

"We'd just entered the tunnel and there it was lying in the water", one of the bargees blurted, "so we dragged it out thinking it was still more crap somebody had chucked in there and… it was a bit of a shock, to tell the truth".

"I've no doubt it was" Hindbuck said as he looked back over his shoulder. "Is that it over there?"

"Yes, sir" Penny replied.

Ethan followed Hindbuck as he wandered over to the P.C., reaching him just as he was covering over the body with a sheet. Hindbuck nodded and he pulled back the sheet to reveal the man's face. It was Billy, the top of his head gone, and his hair taken with it. What was left, was bloody and congealed. Across his face there were cuts and bruises, and his eyes were staring wide open as though he had departed this world in abject terror.

"No native did that" Ethan said.

"I wasn't suggesting they did" replied Hindbuck as he nodded Penny to come over.

"Well, who then?"

Penny handed Hindbuck something or other swathed in cloth. Hindbuck took it from him and carefully unwrapped it. "The man who owns this here is my guess".

"Seen this, before, have you?" he said holding out the object to Ethan. It was a finely carved, bone handled hunting knife. "It was found on the dead body".

"How many more times, I don't know how it got there" Ethan protested.

He was sitting at a rickety table in a dark and dismal interview room back at the police station. Hindbuck was sitting opposite him.

"Is it yours?"

"Yes, yes of course it's mine. Who else would have a knife like that around these parts?"

"Quite. So, how do you explain us finding it on a dead man?"

"I don't know, I don't know how it got there. I didn't even notice it was missing".

Hindbuck stared across the table at Ethan, running his hands through his hair, frustration starting to get the better of him.

"When did you last see it?" he asked.

Ethan sighed exasperated. "I already told you, yesterday afternoon before I went out to the picture show. It was right there on the table next to my bed".

"So, I'll ask you one more time... how come we found it on the body of a dead man?"

"How many more times, I don't know how". He sat forward changing tack. "Just tell me one thing, when, exactly, am I supposed to have done all this?"

"Late last night from what I can gather".

"In that case, all you need to do is speak to Ella. She can vouch for me. After the picture show we headed up to the castle to see the lights. Stayed there until the early hours".

"So I can add trespass to your list of crimes then, can I?"

Ethan frowned questioningly.

"The castle" Hindbuck affirmed. "It's off limits at night... or didn't you notice that when you were climbing over the gate?"

Ethan was irritated at the diversion. Frustrated. "Look, just speak with Ella and I can get outta here" he insisted.

"I already did".

"And?"

"She claims that after the show she said goodnight to you outside the Methodist Hall, and after that went straight home".

"What?"

"That she was in bed just after ten and stayed there until first thing".

"But why, why would she say that?" Ethan exclaimed. "It's just not true".

Hindbuck simply shrugged.

Ethan had started to feel hemmed in, trapped in an alien world he would never understand or would ever care to understand, and he was becoming more and more fraught. His frustration quickly turned to anger. "I want to speak to the Colonel" he demanded through gritted teeth.

"No need to worry about that" Hindbuck assured him nonchalantly. "I already did".

"And?"

"He agrees with me. If a crime has been committed, then it's my duty to deal with it... no matter what the consequences".

Hope crushed, Ethan looked away, devastated that the one person he thought would stand by his side, would be there when he needed him most, had so callously deserted him in his hour of need.

"You've done what?" the Chief Inspector bellowed accusingly as he sat at the desk in his office wearing a face like thunder. "The righthand man of the most recognisable face on the bloody planet and you've got him banged up in a shitty cell not much better than the Black Hole of bloody Calcutta. What the hell were you thinking, man?"

"Just doing my duty, sir. The job you pay me for".

"Bollocks to duty!"

"If a crime has been committed…"

"If a crime has been committed then we have to think of the consequences before we go round accusing folks who might or might not be guilty of something. Not everything is black and white, you know".

"I'm beginning to see that" Hindbuck mumbled philosophically to himself. The Chief just about caught it "Thank fuck for that" he yapped. "About bloody time".

For the next ten minutes or more, Hindbuck stood listening impassive, subjected to his boss's ranting and raving as he spat out every curse and expletive known to man, and quite a few more that hadn't before been invented. All the time he was growing redder and redder in the face and the veins in his neck thickened and pulsated until, just when it seemed certain his blood vessels would burst along with the rest of him, he placed his elbows on the desk in front of him and sank his head into his hands.

Cutting a pitiful figure of desperation, for a couple of minutes he sat breathing erratically and wallowing in the injustice of it all. He had been offered a promotion, a transfer to somewhere there were trees and sunshine and where the only crime was committed by some little old lady who had butchered her dahlias. His patch certainly wouldn't be blighted by a vision of hell just up the road, that was for sure. He sighed long and deep.

"This is the last straw" he said, starting to trot out his much-loved mantra, repeating the same desperate speech he had preached many times before. "When this is all over…"

This time Hindbuck was ready for him. "You needn't bother with all that bollocks" he stated with surprising bluntness as he butted in.

"What did you just say?" the Chief barked astounded at his flagrant insubordination.

"I said, you can quit the bollocks and save your breath. When this is all done and dusted, that's it, I'm finished".

"Finished?"

"Come the end of next month I'll be riding off into the setting sun… if I can find it, that is". Hindbuck had clearly been around Bill Cody far too long and his influence was rubbing off on him. Either that, or he was undeniably inspired by something the wily old frontiersman had said to him.

It was a side of the man standing before him the Chief hadn't seen before. All right, he could be a complete pain in the arse at times, but he'd never before been insubordinate. He was about to say as much when…

"And just in case you're thinking you'll change my mind"

He took a dogeared envelope from his pocket and tossed it onto the desk. "My letter of resignation"

The Chief gazed at the letter sitting on the desk before picking it up like it was a red-hot poker and he was about to get burned. "You… You can't do it. Not just like that" he insisted stuttering.

"Just watch me".

"But who's going to take care of law and order?"

"Not my problem. You'll just have to find some other mug to do it, won't you?"

"What, in that God forsaken hole?" the Chief gasped incredulously. "Who the hell in their right mind would agree to that, for Christ's sake?

"You should have thought about that when I came in here begging for the resources to do the job properly, shouldn't you. Fifteen years, it's been. Just me and two other blokes doing the best we could. Mucking along. Well, not anymore, I'm done".

The Chief had wanted to say more, much more, but all he could manage at the time was "We'll talk more when this is all over".

"I'll leave you a photo" Hindbuck told him.

In one of the dingy, cramped cells at the rear of the police station, a thin shaft of moonlight filtered through the grimed lights of a tiny window high in the wall. It was dismal, it was dusty, and a place hope rarely visited.

It had been three days since Ethan had been arrested, and he was lying forlornly on the hard, wooden slab that misrepresented itself as a bed staring mindlessly up at the ceiling. The bed was shoved into the far corner. A second bed was rammed against the wall on the other side, with just a narrow walkway and a stinking piss pot between them.

Footsteps could be heard approaching down the passage outside and a moment later the cover of a small peephole in the steel door slid open revealing Penny's eyes. "Stand away from the door" the young constable said with newfound authority.

A moment later, the door opened up and Penny appeared in the corridor.

"Do you think that was really necessary?" Ethan questioned scornfully.

Penny lowered his eyes uncomfortably.

Chalky Harris appeared in the doorway, Hindbuck just behind him. "I ain't goin' in there. Not with him" the thug protested fearfully.

"You'll go where I tell you to go" Hindbuck assured him before shoving him inside, Penny stepping into the corridor and slamming the door shut.

Chalky crossed to the second bed, wary, not for even the briefest moment taking his eye off the man spread out on the bed opposite. Ethan ignored him.

Hindbuck came into the office and flopped down on his chair at the desk. Penny followed him in. "Do you think that was wise, sir" he questioned uneasily. "I mean, putting those two in a cell together, isn't it asking for trouble?"

"I'm counting on it" Hindbuck replied.

He sat back in his chair reflecting on the last thing Cody had said to him over the telephone *"Remember, anything you need, just holler"* he had repeated.

Maybe, the time had come.

In the fine dining restaurant of Hambley Hall, Pyke sat at his usual table with two other men, neither of whom appeared particularly comfortable. The first of them was Oliver Bennet. The more senior of the two and the more nervous, Bennett was thick set and his smooth-shaven head shone with perspiration. The other man, Gerald Hawkins, was much lighter, his face so skeletally thin one could be excused for suspecting his wife of being partial to necrophilia. Both men were dressed formally in dark grey dinner suits.

A waiter floated gracefully to the table carrying three plates of food, steak for Pyke, light leafy salad for the gents. He paused. Pyke nodded and he placed the plates down in front of them. "Bon Appetit" he said, bowing his head slightly before quietly retiring.

"So, let me get this straight" Pyke said tucking a napkin scruffily into his collar. "You came all the way down here – to a place where you don't belong and never will, I might add - with the idea of making a few bob by setting up even more factories to pump out even more shit… and now you've lost everything. Right?" He picked up a silver knife and used it to scoop peas from the plate to his mouth.

The two men glanced at one another awkwardly. Bennet a ran finger under his collar. Hawkins nodded.

"And now you want me to bail you out?

Hawkins nodded a second time.

"And why would I want to do that?" Pyke asked, sawing off a slice of steak and stuffing it in his mouth, jowls slobbering. "What's in it for me?"

Hawkins glanced at Bennett who silently nodded his authority before picking up a napkin from the table.

"It's a well-known fact, Mister Pyke" Hawkins continued, "That you already have an interest in the majority of the businesses around here. And by Mister Bennett offering you the opportunity to add to your already extensive portfolio, I feel sure that you…"

"Ah, now I get it", Pyke sneered, prodding his fork at Hawkins but addressing Bennett, "He's you're lapdog, isn't he? The money fiddler"

Hawkins flashed a look at Bennett.

"It's true, yes, I am indeed Mister Bennett's financial advisor" Hawkins replied for the other man as he tried to gain the higher ground, "But rest assured, Mister Pyke, Mister Bennett has granted me carte blanche to negotiate on his behalf… including any financial details that might further our negotiations".

"I bet he has. And does that include what you've got squirreled away so he don't know about it?"

159

Hawkins squirmed.

Pyke took another slice of steak before turning his attention to Bennett. "And what about you, don't you have anything to say on the matter? Or, has the cat got your tongue?"

Bennett did his best to compose himself, clasped his hands together on the tabletop to stop them from shaking.

"I lost everything on that train, Mister Pyke" he started desolately. "My business, my savings... my life. Everything. And if there is any way I can salvage even part of that which I lost, then that is what I shall do. For the sake of my family".

If Pyke was impressed, he made a good fist of not showing it. "Pretty speech, you should think about treading the boards. Might make back some of it back that way" he sneered.

Bennett's shoulders slumped, and he mopped his brow with his napkin. Hawkins sighed and looked away.

"Come on, eat up" Pyke said nodding towards the untouched plates of food in front of each of them. "We'll have bunnies running around all over the place if you leave that stuff lying around".

Realising the conversation was going no further, Bennett picked up a fork and poked his salad, shifting in around his plate. Hawkins didn't bother.

In the dismal, gloomy cell that was scattered in rat's droppings and reeked of animal faeces, Chalky perched on the edge of his bed, edgy and suspicious. "So, what are you suggesting?" he asked warily as his eyes narrowed.

"We call a truce between us and work together".

"And why the fuck would I want to do that?"

"So that we can get outta here".

"Oh, I get it" Chalky smirked, "you're worried you might get a bit of what was coming to young Ella when you nod off".

"I'm sure you're too much of a man for that".

Chalky continued to eye Ethan suspiciously.

"Right, let me get this straight. You and me, we just walk out'f here without so much as a by your leave. And how are we going manage that, exactly? In case you failed to notice, the door's slammed shut and we're bloody well locked in, you saft bugger".

He flopped onto his back and gazed up at the ceiling. "Bloody wazzock!"

"Hold on there, just listen up for a minute" Ethan insisted. "It's simple. When Penny comes to bring us food, we overpower him and slip outta here. By the time anybody notices, it will be too late to do anything about it".

"This ain't the wild west, you know. It ain't one of those movies that ponce is hawking round. Besides, what's Hindbuck going to be doin' all this time? Sitting at his desk scratchin' his bollocks?"

"Hindbuck will be long gone by then. He never hangs around late at night unless he has to. So, what do you think?"

"I think you're a mad man, is what I think" Chalky told him emphatically. "Now. just put your head down and shut the fuck up".

"Suit yourself" Ethan said with a shrug. "Either way, with or without you, I'm outta here".

It was getting late by the time Ethan heard footsteps approaching down the corridor outside. He was on his feet and across the cell in a flash, pressing himself against the wall behind the door.

Chalky looked over and shook his head.

The jangling sound of keys in the lock preceded the door being shoved open and the unsuspecting Penny stepping in carrying a tray on which were two bowls of something that purported to be food.

Before he had the chance to say anything, Ethan had leapt out, grabbed the truncheon from under his tunic and smashed him over the head with it. And as he slammed against the wall out cold, the tray crashed to the floor covering it in murky brown slop.

At the door, Ethan stopped and looked back, "Are you coming, or not?"

Ethan edged along the corridor with his back to the wall, Chalky right behind him equally wary.

As they neared the office door, Ethan turned back to Chalky and put his finger to his mouth. He took a look. The office was empty, and he ran straight to the safe. By good fortune, it had been left unlocked. He pulled open the door and quickly rifled through the contents inside, bringing out his Colt in its holster and his bone handled hunting knife. He belted the holster to his waist and tied the string that attached it to his thigh. Then, his slipped the knife into its scabbard and hurried out, Chalky right behind him.

A moment later Ethan dashed back in, grabbed his hat and Slicker from the coat stand in the corner, and then he was gone again as quickly as he came.

When Ethan came down the steps onto the pavement outside the police station, it was dark... and Chalky was gone. Standing in the dull glow of the lamp over the station door, he looked around urgently, just in time to see his reluctant partner in crime disappear into an alleyway further along the street.

He gave chase.

Hindbuck stepped into the office from the corridor where he had been concealed in one of the cells. And as he stood pensively staring at the door, Penny came out right behind him.

"You alright, lad?" Hindbuck asked.

"Fine, sir" Penny replied nursing the back of his neck, "He caught me across the shoulder, that's all".

"Pity he didn't hit your head. Might have knocked some sense in".

Disappointment clouded Penny's face.

Then Hindbuck smiled and with a quick nod of his head he said, "You did good, lad. Well done". His tone was almost affectionate.

Penny puffed out his chest, thrilled but embarrassed at the first hint of approval from his mentor, the man he aspired to be one day.

CHAPTER 19

In the narrow passageway that was at one moment ominously dark and filled with deep, dark shadow, the next bathed in bursts of brilliant, blinding firelight exploding through the doorways of the small cottage nail shops, foundries, and workshops on either side, Chalky was making his getaway. But although he was good with his fists and handy to have around in a bar brawl, Chalky was never going to come first in the hundred-yard dash, the overhanging precipice that was his beer belly gained curtesy of Nell's nightly hospitality in the Elephant and Castle making sure of that.

Ethan raced along the passageway passing even more narrow arteries on either side as he went. But these were different, these were almost pitch-black corridors that were as potentially dangerous as they were unnerving and unpleasant. At the rear of the flat-faced rows of cottages people called home, they were filled with gloomy nooks and crannies where anyone could easily conceal themselves before springing out and mugging some unsuspecting passer-by returning home with their meagre rations. And they were eerily silent, too; apart from the perpetual thump of the foundry hammers and the occasional screech of a cat or bark of a dog, there was nothing to break the silence other than the sound of Ethan's rapid footfall on the ground.

Without breaking stride, Ethan swept aside one of the rows of washing strung across in front of him, and if he had had time to stop and think about it, he would have wondered what was the point? Why hang out washing that, when it was dry and you took it in, would be so dirty that it needed to go straight back into the washtub?

Up ahead the passageway appeared to come to a dead end, but Chalky stumbled around the corner and disappeared to the left.

Ethan almost slipped as he rounded the corner continuing to give chase, his fancy snakeskin boots with their silver spurs, sliding on the loose, damp gravel under foot. He was greeted by a piece of four by two that loomed from the darkness aimed square at his head. Just in time, as much by instinct as by the speed of his reflexes, the nimble cowboy deftly ducked and, with an ear-splitting crack, the length of timber splintered to smithereens as it smashed against the wall.

The conflict was soon over. Chalky was too exhausted to fight, the exertion of the chase all too much for him. He fell back against the wall and closed his eyes, wheezing as he gasped for air, as he held up his hand in a gesture of submission.

"Alright, there's no need to get nasty" he managed in short, shallow gulps.

Ethan stared deep into the eyes of the thick and heartless goon. "Now, here's what's going to happen" he said in a tone that left little room for debate. "You're going to take me to the place where Jonas Pyke hides himself away in order to orchestrate his nasty little crimes. Understand?"

Chalky hmphed. "Oh aye, and why would I want to do that?" he questioned with renewed defiance. "If I wanted to stick my head in the lion's mouth, I'd go to the circus".

"Because my friend asked you too, that's why".

"Your friend?"

Ethan whipped his sidearm from its holster and cocked the trigger with his thumb pointing the barrel right between Chalky's widening eyes. "I believe you've already met Mister Colt" he said with a half-smile.

Chalky swallowed hard. He was set firmly between the devil and the deep blue sea with not even the remotest possibility of escape, and he knew it.

Every footstep echoed in the cavernous space of the warehouse as Ethan and Chalky strode through the dusty air towards the iron stairs leading up to the nauseating hovel Pyke called home.

"He's not going to like this. Comin' here unannounced" Chalky warn as they climbed the stairs, his voice cracking.

"Let me worry about that" Ethan told him.

As was to be expected, Pyke was in his usual place slouched slovenly behind his desk, his bounteous backside overflowing so as to all but conceal the chair he sat on. Jacko glued to his side like an obedient puppy as they went silently through the papers spread out in front of them. Tommy and Abel were hanging around bored. Hearing footsteps on the stairs, the Staffie got up and started to bark. Pyke dispatched it to the corner with his boot before he nodded to Jacko and the hulk lumbered over to stand behind the door.

Chalky hesitated, not taking his eyes off Ethan as he went to rap on the door. Before he had chance, Ethan reached out and grabbed his hand. Shook his head.

The door opened and Chalky came in. Jacko relaxed, and not realising imminent threat lurking went back to the desk.

"Forgotten how to knock, have you, Chalky?"

Ethan stepped in behind him.

Pyke stared at him hard, "You do know that if you disturb a lion in its den, it's likely to open its gob and bite you?"

Ethan remained unflinching.

"It weren't my idea, Pykie. He has a gun. He made me do it" Chalky blurted fearfully.

"Do what?"

"Bring him here".

"And you think him threatening to put a bullet through your brain is preferable to pissing me off and risking a bloody and excruciating end, do you?"

Pyke watched Chalky squirm.

Ethan was distracted, taken aback at seeing Ella sitting cowed in the corner, and for the briefest moment, before she turned away, her empty eyes met his.

"There's no point looking at her" Pyke assured him scornfully, "She ain't goin' to help you".

Ethan composed himself.

"So, are you goin' to tell me what you're doin' here invading my privacy, or do I have to get Jacko here to beat it out'f you?" Pyke asked, his voice filled with disdain.

"That won't be necessary" Ethan replied cold and unflinching. "I'm here to offer you a proposal".

"Hear that, lads?" Pyke scoffed with a snort that passed as a laugh, "Pretty boy here has a proposal for me. Ain't nobody told him I'm already married?"

The goons laughed out of duty and Ethan wondered who it might be that would be so desperate as to willingly declare '*until death do us part*' to a man so devoid of any basic human decency.

"Oh aye, and what would that be?" Pyke asked once he had controlled his mirth.

Ethan looked around at the other men sitting in the room. Then back to Pyke.

"You lot can all piss off" Pyke said bluntly before turning to Ella. "And you. You can go an' all rather than sitting there all day long scratching your fanny".

Ella stood up and followed Tommy and Abel out, pausing only to look Ethan in the eye. Chalky was the last scurry away, relieved at not having incurred more of Pyke's wrath. A lucky escape.

"I could cheerfully blow that man's brain out'f the back of his head" Ethan declared quietly to himself, but not so quietly that Pyke couldn't hear.

"Oh aye, and why's that then?"

"Remember I told you about the incident in town just after I arrived?"

"What about it?" Pyke's asked, his interest peaked.

"The man who attacked the young lady, Ella. It was him, he was the one."

"Chalky?"

Ethan nodded.

"Was it now" Pyke reflected before quickly changing the subject. "Go on then" he said suddenly indifferent, "this proposal you've got for me, spit it out".

He watched warily through the narrow slits of his beady eyes, as Ethan grabbed a chair, put it down in front of his desk and sat down. Took off his hat and put it down on the table between them.

"The robbery the other night" he said.

"What about it?" Pyke questioned.

"It's one thing getting your hands on something, it's another thing disposing of it".

"And?"

"That's where I might be able to help".

"Always supposing the thieving has anything to do with me, that is".

"It's my understanding everything that happens around these parts has something to do with you, Mister Pyke... one way or another" Ethan insisted.

Pyke examined the cowboy's face, looking for a sign of weakness, a flicker in his eyes to suggest something untoward, some ulterior motive. But there was none. "Go on" he said warily.

"Let's just suppose for one minute a man had come into possession of something that didn't belong to him and he wanted to dispose of it. That might be difficult with the law hanging around. But if that man had a sure-fire way of moving the goods without arousing suspicion, then..." his voice tailed off with a shrug.

Pyke stared at him mystified, "Are you taking the piss, or what? You waltz in here all high and mighty and start blethering bullshit about some bloke who might or might not have something he wants to shift... and you expect me to be impressed? Well, I ain't, and if that's the best you have to offer, then you can fuck off right now".

"There's nothing more I can say" Ethan admitted, "Not until I find a man who's in that position and could do with some help. I just thought you might be able to point me in the right direction".

"Right, well I'll bear that in mind" Pyke told him dismissively, "should I come across him".

Ethan stood up and grabbed his hat, "Well, thanks for your time, Mister Pyke" he said tipping his hat.

He headed for the door. Pyke called him back.

"Hold on a minute, not so quick"

Ethan turned back to face him.

170

"Just for reference, if I do come across this fictious bloke, and if he's in any way interested in what you've got to say, what is it you're suggesting? Not that I'm saying I do, mind".

Ethan came back to the desk and sat down. "When we left here after the show, we were forced to leave some things behind in storage. So, while I was locked away in the stinking pit of a prison cell, I got to thinking, if I could round up some of the men from the show who, with the right incentive, could be guaranteed not to ask any questions, I could arrange to ship out any misappropriate merchandise that needs moving along with it and nobody would be any the wiser".

"And why can't I... he do that himself without the bother of all your crap? Why can't he just load up a cart, slap the horse's arse and drive it out'f here?".

"Because he would be caught before he'd even left town" Ethan insisted.

"Oh aye, and what gives you that idea?" Pyke hmphed derisively.

"Because they already have men guarding every exit outta here in anticipation of your man doing exactly that".

Pyke's eyes narrowed and his brow furrowed. This was news to him. Had his network of informers broken down? Momentarily he had been caught off guard, and in those rare times there was only one defence – bravado.

"So what, there's always the cut"

Ethan frowned quizzically.

"The cut... the canal" Pyke told him like he was talking to a simpleton.

"The cut. Right" Ethan repeated bemused. "They have that covered too".

Pyke once again searched Ethan's eyes for any hint of deceit. He didn't find any. "And how come you're so smart all of a sudden?"

"The chief inspector has a loud voice when he's angry.

"The chief inspector?"

"I heard him reading the riot act to Hindbuck back at the police station. Seems this incident with the train being robbed has a lot of people spooked, not least the chief inspector who feels it might jeopardise the promotion he's put in for".

There it was at last, something for Pyke to latch onto. He'd heard the Chief had put in for a transfer and would soon be moving on, and here was confirmation. Maybe the cowboy was speaking the truth. Not that it made him any less suspicious.

"Go on" he urged cautiously.

"Whatever it was that was on that train must've been pretty valuable, not just the bunch of cash and a few bonds you might have expected, and they need it retrieving before the shit hits the fan".

"And Hindbuck?"

"He's been promised all the manpower he needs to ensure it happens. It's my understanding from what I heard that detachments from forces outside the county – Shropshire, Worcester, is it? The names mean nothing to me – have already been put on alert, and over the next few days they will be rounding up every man that ever committed a crime in the town, and interrogating them, putting pressure on them to see who will crack and let something slip. It's already started. Chalky Harris was hauled in just after I overheard all this… and for no apparent reason from what I can tell".

"Apart from molesting somebody on the street".

"They don't know about that far as I know".

"Did he tell 'em anything?"

Ethan shook his head, "I managed to get him outta there before they had the chance of talking with him. There's another thing too. But for the train robbery there's no way I would have been arrested like I was, not on such thin evidence, the Colonel would have seen to it".

He stood up about to leave. "Anyways, I'd better get outta here, find somewhere to bunk down for the night"

"Where do I find you?" Pyke asked, quickly adding "if I hear of anybody".

"You don't. You just leave a card in the window of the shop opposite the pub and I'll come to you".

"Saying what?"

"That you have a wash tub for sale. Left to you by your grandmother".

He started to leave.

"Hold up, we ay finished here yet", Pyke called after him, his eyebrows creasing with suspicion. "You ay said what's in it for you yet".

Ethan looked back, "That's easy. Revenge".

Pyke tipped his head slightly.

"Out west when a man is falsely accused, he either hires a lawyer, hot foots it outta there like a coward, or he takes matters into his own hands and deals with the problem himself. No matter which way, he doesn't just sit there and let those in authority make a scapegoat out'f him. Personally, I favour the third option".

And with that, he tipped his hat and was gone.

After a moment, Pyke struggled to his feet and lumbered over to the window, pondering on what Ethan had said as he watched him stride across the floor below. He was getting thoroughly pissed off by people presuming they knew his business and then telling him what to do with it. First it was the bloke back in the restaurant blubbering like a wench just because he'd lost a few quid, and now the bloody cowboy was sticking his oar in. But at least the cowboy had a motive; revenge. He liked that, revenge, it was his kind of justice, much better than being a goody two shoes and doing the right thing. Doing the right thing, that was all for show. Revenge, that was a real man's motivation. But it didn't add credence to the rest of what Ethan had told him, that could be total bullshit for all he knew. On the other hand... what if he was right? What if the authorities really had blockaded the place preventing him from shifting his ill-gotten gains? What if the tide really was turning against him? No matter what, there was no point taking any chances.

"Find Chalky and check out his story" he instructed Jacko who had come to stand next to him, "and, if the cowboy's telling the truth, just make sure the gobshite scar face knows to keep his gob shut. Oh aye, and that other thing, the thing out by the station, check that out an' all while you're at it. I'd forgotten about that".

"And if it was him?"

"Then he's gonna have to pay, isn't he".

Jacko nodded and headed for the door.

"Hang on a minute, I ay finished yet" Pyke called after him abruptly.

Jacko stopped and waited.

"When that's done, get out there and see if they really have blockaded the place. I doubt it, they don't have the manpower, but we can't take any chances. And when you've done that, find out if they really do have all that circus crap stashed away. We might need it".

Jacko left, leaving Pyke to ponder alone, wondering just what the world was coming to when the authorities started to get the upper hand.

It didn't bear thinking about.

CHAPTER 20

Later that evening, in the office of the police station, Hindbuck sat with Ethan, one on either side of his desk. It was the perfect place for the cowboy to hide away, after all, who would think of looking for an escaped felon in the very place he had been incarcerated in. He could easily sneak in and out of the building without being seen and bunk down in one of the cells at night, and if he was unfortunate enough to be witnessed creeping back in and somebody came calling, Hindbuck had the perfect excuse for him being there. All he had to say was he caught him sneaking back in for something he had left behind, and he had arrested him. Job done.

Hindbuck poured them both a drink, whiskey for himself and bourbon from a bottle Nell had somehow managed to get her hands on for Ethan. Just how things so rare magically materialised in the town was a total mystery to him. One day he would have to find out. Then again, it may be best if he didn't know.

"Here" he said as he slid the glass across the desk. "Looks like you need it".

"Thanks" Ethan replied as he picked up the glass and sipped from it, remembering back to the night he had been arrested.

***

In the office back at the police station. Hindbuck was interviewing Ethan, the bone handle knife on the table between them.

Ethan had started to feel hemmed in, trapped in an alien world he would never understand, and he was becoming more and more fraught. He had to get out of there. He had to do something. Find the real murderer. Something. Anything. "I want to speak to the Colonel" he suddenly insisted.

"No need to worry about that" Hindbuck assured him, "I already did".

"And?"

"He agrees with me. If a crime has been committed, then it's my duty to deal with it... no matter what the consequences".

Hope crushed, Ethan looked away, devastated that the one person he thought would stand by his side, would be there when he needed him most, had so callously deserted him in his hour of need.

"If Pyke really has moved on from just harassing innocent local folk and snatching their livelihoods, or banging a few heads together, then he needs to be stopped before it gets out'f hand"

"What are you saying? Ethan queried.

"We take the fight to him"

"So why arrest me?"

"Justice has to be seen to be done in order to maintain the impression we know what we're doing, whether it is or not has bugger all to do with it. Besides, you'll need an excuse for when you go calling on him".

"You arrested me just so that it looked good?" Ethan asked in disbelief. "And now want me to infiltrate Pyke's operation and help you bring him to justice?"

"That's about the size of it".

"And whose bright idea was this… No, don't tell me… the Colonel?"

Hindbuck tipped his head and bobbed his shoulders.

"Says it might make a fitting swansong"

"I should've guessed" Ethan hmphed.

***

Hindbuck had gone on to tell Ethan of his frustration at not being able to move against Pyke, lacking the resources and backing of his superiors who had steadfastly refused to sanction any such support in the mistaken belief that the place was a hellhole and best left to sort itself out. All Hindbuck had to do was keep a lid on it. And, with the assistance of two constables, one of whom had to be seconded in on a needs basis, he had managed to do just that, while all the time Pyke continued harassing, blackmailing, extorting, and causing grievous bodily harm to anybody that so much as looked at him, all with little risk of retribution. It was an intolerable situation and one which had constantly driven the detective to distraction. But despite all that, he had carried out his duties as best he could, soldiering on in the resolute belief that the hard working, God fearing people of the Black Country deserved better than the cards fate had cruelly dealt them. Much better. But this latest incident had changed all that. No longer was 'keeping a lid on it' a viable option.

The robbery of the train had witnessed a change of direction, an escalation in the activities of the unprincipled Pyke dynasty, although he doubted that even Pyke had got wind of what was being transported along with cash and bonds on the train. More likely he came across the treasure trove by glorious happenchance.

Whereas his previously criminal transgressions had been confined to the town and its immediate surrounds, Pyke was now spreading his wings... and they needed clipping before they grew feathers and he learned to fly.

But if Hindbuck was to bring down the obnoxious criminal overlord, then he was on his own. The Chief Inspector, concerned more with his image than he was local affairs - having his head so far up his arse as Hindbuck put it – did not, or would not, accept for even a moment that Pyke's latest escapade potentially had far more dire consequences than keeping a gregarious showman happy by letting his right-hand man get away with what was potentially murder. No matter how famous he might be. As for the train, he was so much focussed on his idyllic future in the countryside, the magnitude of the robbery had eluded him completely. The man was a stork.

"So, what is it that's in those crates? You were going to tell me earlier." Ethan asked taking a sip of the Bourbon.

"Anglo-Saxon gold and silver. Some lucky bastard discovered it hidden away in a cave under the castle. Worth a King's ransom, from what I'm told".

"How long had it been there?"

"Nobody knows, or how it got there. Not that they were the primary target for Pyke I shouldn't imagine. That would have been the cash and papers, promissory notes, bonds, and debentures, that sort of thing".

"And the artefacts were a bonus?"

Hindbuck nodded. "Way out of Pyke's league, that's for sure. Which is why I think he might have trouble moving them".

It was dark and deathly silent, the silence broken only by the fearsome screech of wide, heavy steel doors being dragged across the floor. With the doors open, defused moonlight spilled through and across the warehouse floor. On two sides, wooden crates were stacked two high. There were still more crates at the back.

Jacko slipped in with Tommy and Abel. They were each carrying heavy, black iron crowbars.

"Right, get to it" Jacko instructed waving the offensive weapon around. "And make sure you shut them up proper when you're done, we don't want nobody knowing we've been in here. Understand?".

Tommy and Abel acquiesced with a nod of the head, and the three men set to work carefully prising open the crates and examining their contents. It was nearly an hour before they found what they were looking for.

"Over here" Tommy shouted, a note of triumph in his voice.

The other two men went over. Inside the crate there were costumes and an assortment of props from the show, hats, breeches, horse's tackle, and some of the golden balls that they had tossed into the air before some sure shot shattered them.

"There's another over here" Abel said having gone to work on another of the dusty crates close by. "Full of the same stuff".

"Right, that's it, then. Just fasten em up and let's get out'f here" Jacko instructed, "And remember, careful how you go about it".

"So, what happened with Pyke?" Hindbuck asked as he poured them each another shot.

"Pretty much the way we talked about it. Claimed he knew nothing about anything. So I just laid the bait and... Ella was there too".

Hindbuck slid his drink across the desk. "I wouldn't think too badly of her. She has to live around here. A few days, and you'll be gone"

"I don't".

Hindbuck frown quizzically.

"Think badly of her. It's just that..." he was struggling to find the words. "I don't know, she's just gotten under my skin".

"Hormones are funny like that... so they tell me" Hindbuck said sitting back. "Me, I wouldn't know. Been a bachelor all my life". He took a sip. "It's the job. Not knowing if you're going to come home at the end of a shift, or if you do what state you'll be in. I wouldn't want to put any woman through that".

"It's not like that" Ethan said reflectively. "I just feel... I don't know, like I have to do something to help her escape from all she has to suffer here".

"There's nothing you can do" Hindbuck assured him, "short of taking her with you when you go".

"You don't think I haven't already thought about that?" Ethan told him.

Hindbuck reflected a while before quickly changing the subject. "Anyway" he said, "All that might change once we've dealt with Pyke and he's brought to account. Until such time he has to be our sole priority".

Ethan nodded distantly.

Jacko made his way cautiously up the hillside. Out of the town, in the woodland, the moon had chance to shine and was peeping through light drifting cloud and filtering down through the branches and leaves of the trees in radiant beams. There was the occasional sound of wildlife too, something scurrying away in the undergrowth, the stifled cry of a nocturnal animal calling for its mate.

As he picked his way slowly towards the flickering light ahead, Jacko was careful not to make a sound, mindful that just one misplaced step, the crack of a branch under foot, could be the early warning that led to him being discovered.

When he had crept as close as he dared, he concealed himself behind one of the knotted and gnarled trunks, peeping out just enough so that he could see but not be seen.

Fifty yards ahead in a small clearing, several men sat around a campfire talking. He couldn't hear what they were saying, nor could he make out who they were, to him they were no more than dark silhouettes against the dancing red flames of the fire. But it was enough to confirm what he was there for and he quietly turned around and made his way back towards the town.

Hindbuck downed his drink, stood up and grabbed his greatcoat from the hat stand. "Time for me to head off home, I think. And for you to get some shut eye. With any luck there's a big day ahead of us tomorrow.

"Night" he said heading out of the door.

Ethan waved, sat in quiet contemplation.

CHAPTER 21

The small kitchen of the house that Ella shared with her father was depressingly gloomy, defused half-light filtering in through the cheap, thread bear curtains hanging from a cord held up by nails that stretched across the top of the window. Under the window there was a single, white enamelled cast iron sink, and in the centre of the room, sitting in the middle of a battered wooden table, an oil lamp that cast shadows around the room, provided what little true illumination there was. Two places were set for dinner, a fork and spoon sitting on either side of chipped and cracked plates.

Resting against one wall there was an equally battered dresser. Scattered haphazardly on it were three plates and several pieces of blemished china. Against a second wall, there was a black iron stove with a black flue pipe that rose up through the ceiling. Sitting on top of the stove was an enamel cooking pot and a cheap galvanised kettle that whistled as the water inside it came to the boil.

Ella was standing over the cooking pot stirring the contents when Nobby came in wearing just his baggies and what was once a white vest. His braces hung loose at his sides. "Ain't that ready yet? he bellyached almost before he was through the door. He pulled out one of two rickety chairs at the table and flopped down carelessly on one of them. "My belly feels like me throats been cut"

"It'll be five minutes" Ella told him.

"About time. After that I think we should have some fun… don't you? End the day off nice"

Ella felt a shiver run down her spine. She knew only too well what fun meant.

"I'm going out" she answered quickly.

"You can go out when I say you can and not before" Nobby told her in no uncertain terms. "Pyke will just have to wait for once".

Ella didn't argue. There was no point?

Eager to discover the truth about the stolen knife, and even though he suspected he already knew the answer, Ethan waited in the shadows that filled one of the narrow alleys behind the shops for Ella.

Across from him there was a narrow passageway between the houses, and from his vantage point he could make out a woman working in a small nail shop. Working bare breasted, her hair stacked up on top of her head and with a leather apron tied around her waist, she hammered the small glowing rods of iron out on a blackened anvil before picking them up with pincers and plunging them into the tub of dirty water next to her. A cloud of steam engulfed her before slowly dispersing.

It had started to rain, a light rain the likes of which can soak you to the skin without you even knowing it. Off in the distance, a dog barked and a moment later the air was filled by the sound of a cat screeching.

As Ethan shivered uncomfortably and turned the collar of his Slicker against the cold, he began to wonder. Maybe she wasn't coming home that night. Maybe she rarely came home at night. Maybe, just maybe, she was locked away with Pyke somewhere and couldn't get away or tucked up in his bed already. Fast asleep hopefully. The thought sickened him. He could barely think about it, every time he did, he felt a tightening in his stomach and the almost irresistible urge to throw up.

He stamped his feet and blew warming air into his cupped hands. Perhaps it was time to leave, time to accept what was meant to be. Or was it? Just when he had made his decision, he heard the hurried trip of dainty booted feet running across cobbled stones and, a moment later, Ella burst out from the yard at the rear of the house. And as she ran past him with her hood up to shield her from the rain, he stepped out and took her arm.

Ella let out an involuntary gasp, "You shouldn't be here, you have to go" she implored him.

"Not until I have some straight answers" Ethan replied forcefully.

"Are you alright out there, Ella" the woman called from the nail shop.

Ella hesitated before replying, her voice cracking "Yes, yes I'm fine, Florrie. Nothing to worry about".

Without looking directly at him, she shrugged off Ethan's hand impatiently, "We have to get out'f here" she said urgently as she started up the alleyway.

Ethan didn't protest, just followed her as they made their way through a maze of gloomy alleys so tight, they were almost as oppressive as the canal tunnel. And, as they stepped out onto the canal towpath, she turned on him. "What the fuck do you think you're doing" she spat at him furiously. "Anybody sees us together and I'm a dead woman. You an' all most likely. Or don't you give a shit?"

In that moment Ethan felt guilty. But it was a guilt filled with rage. Anger that one so young should feel that way, not feeling able to be seen with anybody, not just him, anybody. To be in such fear for her life.

"Now, just fuck off and leave me alone" she said bitterly, turning away so she didn't have to look at him.

"I'm sorry…" Ethan started not having chance to say more before she had turned on him once again,

"Sorry? It's all right being sorry. Being sorry is goin' to do me a fat lot of good when I'm lying dead in my coffin, isn't it"

Ethan didn't know what to say, standing dumbstruck.

Ella stared at him from under her hood "You still don't get it, do you?" she sneered. "You… me. It was all one big act, Pyke's way of keeping you out of the road while him and his mates went about their business".

"But why?"

"Because you had to start poking your bleedin' nose in other people's business, that why. Turning up at the fight stirring up trouble. It was all right when you were goin' to be gone the next day, but Chalky and his mates beating the shit out'f you meant you were goin' to be hanging around until you recovered, and he wasn't about to take any chances".

Ethan took a deep breath and ran his hands through his hair. "This is madness" he declared bereft of belief. "And the knife?"

"My dad's idea. Said he owed you and if I got him the knife, he could stich you up. Make sure you paid".

"He'd do that? He'd kill a man and slice off the top of his head just to get even with me... and all because I wouldn't give him a job?"

"Looks like it" Ella replied with a dismissive shrug of her shoulders.

Ethan stood in a state of shock, his head reeling with each and every sordid revelation, the whole world he found himself unwillingly thrust into totally alien to him. It was like he was living a nightmare. "Before I leave here, I'm going to make them pay" he declared unequivocally. "Every one of them".

"Oh yeah, goin' to go chargin' in on your hoss and give 'em all a right seeing to, are you?" Ella mocked scornfully. "You and whose army?"

Ethan didn't reply. He wanted to say more but couldn't, not right then. But when this was all over...

"I think I'd better go" he said quietly.

"You do that. Piss off back to wherever it is you come from" Ella huffed before adding derisively mocking, "The wide-open plains, and pretty little streams or whatever it is you're so bleedin' fond of".

She turned away from him.

For a few moments, Ethan observed her in silence, then he turned away and walked off back along the tow path. He had gone only a few paces when a piercing scream broke the night air. He spun around and...

Ella had fallen to her knees and was clutching her belly, rocking back and forth. He rushed to her side and dropped to his haunches next to her. She was inconsolable, unable to speak through her tears, the sobs, her pitiful whimpers punctuated by short, desperate cries of agony. It was like watching a wounded animal baying before being shot to put it out of its misery.

"What is it, what's wrong?" Ethan asked reaching out and placing a hand on her shoulder.

Ella couldn't reply, overcome by the agonising waves of pain. He reached under her hood to stroke her brow and offer her some comfort, gasping when her saw her bruised and battered face.

"I'll kill him" he declared way beyond angry.

Ella let out yet another blood curdling scream. He looked down and where her cloak had parted, he could see the blood streaming down her legs and onto the ground, diluted by the constantly falling rain as it trailed across the towpath before drip dripping into the canal.

Ella screamed again and not knowing what else to do, he swept her up into his arms and carried her away.

189

Ethan looked down at Ella's blood still wet on his hands and on his Slicker, and instantly felt a surge of hopelessness swell over him like a tidal wave. When he had arrived at the station, Penny, who was on night shift holding the fort in case of any emergency, had been dozing in a chair, immediate ran round to Hindbuck's place and brought him back. The aging detective hadn't been best pleased at being woken from his sleep by someone hammering so loudly on his door at that time of night, but when he saw the state of the girl, all that was forgiven. Immediately, he rushed her to the infirmary and all Ethan could do was wait.

Penny sat and watched as Ethan paced up and down waiting for news. Every now he would stop and then let out a deep sigh of anguish before running his hands through his hair.

Hindbuck returned about fifteen minutes later and Ethan was on him like a shot. "Well?"

"It doesn't look good" the detective replied mournfully. "She's lost a lot blood and is as weak as a kitten. Right now, they have her drugged up to the eyeballs, so we won't know more until later".

"And the baby?"

Hindbuck shook his head. "The beating saw to that".

"I'll kill him" Ethan repeated, incandescent with rage as he started for the door.

"No wait" Hindbuck said sharply, grabbing his arm to stop him leaving. "Take the time to think about it".

"I've already thought about it".

"And the consequences if you do?"

Ethan remained unflinching, still seething, inhaling, and exhaling in short, sharp breaths.

"If you go charging in now, everything we've set in place will be wasted and Pyke will get away with it like he always does" the policeman told him.

Ethan's breathing slowly evened.

"If you wait a bit longer, Pyke will get his comeuppance and… you can think about dealing with Nobby when it's all done. Just leave it for now".

Ethan considered for a few moments in wild eyed silence. Then he said quietly "I want to see her".

Despite Hindbuck's protestations to the contrary, the policeman finally agreed, but only on the proviso that Ethan abide by his strict rules. When they arrived at the infirmary, he was to wait across the street while Hindbuck went inside and checked the coast was clear.

So, he waited.

His mind was racing, the unfathomable connection between him and Ella running so deep it hurt. How had a young woman, so often as coarse as a rowdy ranch hand, come to get under his skin the way she had? And in such a short time. Was it infatuation? Was it love? Or was it simply an overwhelming sense of pity for someone whose life was so devoid of hope? Whatever it was, he knew one thing for certain; he had met someone for whom he would gladly risk his life for if it meant saving hers.

The lights in a window of the infirmary flashed twice, the predetermined sign he and Hindbuck had agreed to signal that all was clear. One quick look to make certain that nobody was around, and then he stepped out of the shadow and started across the street.

Ethan came in through the back entrance of the infirmary, away from the prying eyes that might spot him and raise the alarm. Gone were his Slicker and distinctive ten-gallon hat, replaced by the dark blue uniform and 'custodian' hard hat of the constabulary. It was a look they had conceived before they left the station. That way, hopefully, if anyone were to catch sight of Ethan, then the observer wouldn't be able to say with any degree of certainty who it was they had seen, just that they were wearing a police uniform. P.C. Penny, perhaps, Hindbuck would argue.

He hurried along to where Hindbuck was standing alert at Ella's door, anxious as he looked first one way and then the other. He was about to go in, when Hindbuck took his arm. "Five minutes and no more" the policeman warned him sternly. "Understand? Not one second more".

Ethan nodded his agreement and slipped inside, closing the door behind him.

Ethan thought he had prepared himself for what to expect, but the sight of Ella lying with her eyes closed, heavily drugged and barely conscious, in the hospital bed over by the window still came as a shock. Even in the dimmed light of the room he could make out the heavy bruise on her cheek that was already darkening to purple and the red swelling around her eye turning to jelly.

He quietly made his way across the room and sat down on a hard-backed chair next to the bed. Ella didn't even realise he was there, not until he gently took her hand when she forced open her eyes. And as she did so, Ethan thought for a moment he detected the faintest of smiles, but then it was gone, replaced by tiredness and exhaustion.

"Who did this to you?" he ventured quietly as he tenderly stroked her hair, "Was it him? Was it Pyke?"

"Leave it. It's done now" Ella managed in short, gasped breaths, her chest rising and falling increasingly irregularly, "No good will come of it. Not now. If you really want to help me, just sit there and tell me about where you come from".

Ethan hesitated before starting to paint a vivid picture of his beloved homeland, a picture so colourful and glowing, as she closed her eyes and listened, Ella could almost picture herself being there, feel the warm sunshine on her face and the breeze gently caressing her skin as she gazed up at an endless sea of blue. He told her of the wild open plains stretching as far as the eye could see, the dry, prairie shortgrass scattered across it. He told her of mountains so high they almost touched the fluffy soft clouds drifting above them, and of mountain streams, the water so crystal clear you could easily see it swirling around the stones on the bed and the fish wriggling around them. And when he was done...

193

"I wish I could see it" Ella managed.

"You will one day".

"Oh aye, and one day pigs might fly"

"One day I will take you there, I promise. You have my word on it".

Hindbuck stuck his head around the door, "Time to go" he said.

"I'll make Pyke pay for what he's done to you. He won't get away with it. Not this time".

Ella turned away so as not to witness the sickening look of revulsion that would surely cloud his face when she told him. "It weren't Pyke" she whispered

"Who then?"

"Me dad… when I told him no. That if he was that desperate, he could go down the whorehouse".

"And the baby? That was his too?"

Ella nodded, clearly feeling a deep sense of shame.

Ethan couldn't bring himself to believe what he was hearing. The debauched depravity of a man that would do such things and to his own flesh and blood, to his only daughter, the person he was supposed to be there to protect. It was all too much to take in. The very thought sickened him to the core, and he felt like throwing up.

"I said, we have to go" Hindbuck snapped. "Now".

Earlier, Hindbuck had confided in Nell, telling her of the arrangement Ethan had with Pyke over the postcard and asking her to look out for it.

When they arrived back at the station, dawn was already breaking, and Penny, who had been on duty overnight, was there waiting for them with news. In the early hours, Nell had popped in to say the postcard had appeared in the shop window. She knew it was late, but she'd noticed it when she was locking up and thought the inspector would want to know right away.

"That's it, then, we're on" Hindbuck said.

Penny went over to the hat stand, picked off Ethan's Slicker and handed it to him. "I cleaned the blood off as best I could" he said a little self-consciously, "you wouldn't want to be going off into battle dressed like one of the locals, would you?"

Ethan took the Slicker, touched by the other man's kind thought. He nodded a thank you.

Hindbuck gave a satisfied smile. His charge was fast growing into a man. *One day soon*", he thought to himself".

CHAPTER 22

"So, what's the plan?" Pyke asked as he slouched in his chair looking sternly across at Ethan sitting on the other side of the desk

Ethan glanced at Jacko sitting silently by the grotesque lump's side and then back to Pyke. "We transfer the goods to the wagons later this afternoon, just before dusk" he replied.

"Then what?"

"We bring them back here to where it's just a short hop to the railroad. Once it drops dark, we take them over to the yard where my men will be waiting to load them onto the train last minute. We should be done by midnight with any luck."

"Luck don't come into it. Not if you've done your job proper" Pyke told him, making it sound much more like a threat than a mere statement.

"There is one other thing though?"

"Oh aye, and what's that then?"

"The crate containing the artefacts".

"What about it?"

"Where is it?"

"You let me worry about the crate with the artefacts" Pyke assured him haughtily. "When the time comes it'll be where it should be. Until then you've no need to worry about it".

"I just thought…"

"Well don't!" Pyke jumped in, "Just you stick to your job, I'll stick to mine and we'll all be happy – all right?

In truth, there was every need for Ethan to worry about it. Without it being there when the action took place later that night, all of their careful planning went straight out of the grimy window. Pyke would escape Scott free - no doubt be bleating about police harassment and demanding compensation while he was at it - the insurance company would be paying out huge sums for the loss of the priceless items of silver and gold and Hindbuck would have sacrificed his job for nothing.

"Right, well I'm outta here" Ethan declared getting to his feet. "I'll see you tonight".

When he had left, Pyke turned to Jacko. "Make sure you keep your eye on him tonight. We might need his help, for now at least, that don't mean to say I have to trust the bugger".

"And if he steps out of line?"

"You have to ask that, do you?" Pyke sniffed.

Jacko blinked twice, a strong reaction for one who spoke so few words.

Later that afternoon in the office of the police station, Hindbuck was preparing Penny for what was to come. It was important that they got the timing just right in order to make sure Pyke was around when they made their move, if he wasn't, then smarmy shit would squirm his way out of it by claiming it had nothing to do with him and they would have the devil's job proving any different.

"… and when you see them start to round 'em up, that's when you come in with the maria. Not a minute sooner or it will tip 'em off and blow the whole thing. Understand?" Hindbuck finished saying.

The young constable nodded his agreement.

Hindbuck look him in the eye. "You are ready for this, son?" he asked with concern.

"Yes, sir" Penny replied. "Like you once told me, a bloke has to man up sooner or later. If he don't, then he ain't a man".

Hindbuck smiled. Hearing someone at the door, he turned to look, frowning anxiously. A moment later, a man he didn't recognise stepped in.

"Can I help you?" he asked.

"I understand you've been looking for me. Joe O'Malley" the stranger replied.

At no more than five feet six inches tall and stocky without being overweight, the man's dusky coloured skin was framed by long, lank, jet black hair. Thick bushy eyebrows hovered on top of his heavily hooded eyes.

Seeing Hindbuck's querysome look, he smiled. "You probably know me better as Dark Cloud. My father was an Irishman with a sense of humour and wanted to call me Dog Shitting, but my mother objected".

"Your mother was a native Indian?"

"Blackfoot. My father met her while he was bison hunting with the Colonel, got an itch and... well, here I am".

It turned out that while Joe was in town with the show, he had met a young woman named Ida and fallen for her hook line and sinker. When the show got to Liverpool, he was pining for her so much he couldn't take it, so he slipped away and returned to the Black Country to set up home with her.

"It was just after that that I met Pyke", Joe continued, "The vile creature was convinced I could teach one of this henchmen to scalp somebody".

"But why? Why would he want you to do that?"

"From what I can gather, he thought bodies turning up dead and scalped would throw you off the scent should he want to get rid of somebody. The man's deranged. Madder than a trapped rattlesnake".

"So, what happened?"

Joe hmphed derisively, "I told him what he could do, and he said he would get one of his men to do it anyway. He wasn't happy about it and made all kind of threats, so me and Ida made ourselves scarce until he calmed down. We only got back this morning".

He paused to reflect, "Don't know why he should pick on me, I have trouble peeling a prickly pear let alone chopping the top off somebody's head. Must be the colour of my skin".

"And the fact he thinks your name is Dark Cloud" Hindbuck added dryly.

"I suppose there is that" Joe agreed.

Apart from his own men, Pyke had enlisted the help of a number of others, all of them dressed in their uniforms of collarless shirts and baggy trouser held up by leather or cloth braces, to load up the wagons with the items left over from the show. None of them was particularly fond of the fat oaf, nor would they willingly go out of their way to help him. Not under normal circumstances. But when the man was offering a pittance that would put food on the tables of their families for an evening's work, it was an offer they couldn't refuse.

Ethan was standing on the back of one of the wagons supervising. "Bring that one over here" he called to Tommy, Abel and two other men who were manhandling one of the wooden crates close to him.

They each took a corner of the crate.

"When I count to three lift the bugger up" Abel instructed bossily,

The men mumbled their agreement, bent their knees, and braced themselves as they awaited his count".

"Ready".

They took the strain.

"One... two... three"

Their teeth were chattering worse than chimps in a zoo as they lifted crate off the ground, their grunts, and groans in chorus with those being issued by many of those working around them. And as they straightened and lifted, the crate wobbled at one corner and almost toppled over.

"For fuck's sake, watch what you're doing" Tommy chided the man responsible.

"Argh" the man moaned as he strained harder.

The carried the crate across the floor to the wagon, and once it was there, gave it the extra lift it needed to get it onto its edge. Then the four of them got behind it, put their shoulders in and shoved as hard as they could until it was safely on board.

Tommy flopped his back against the side of the wagon. "Bloody hell, that was heavy" he exhaled with relief as he took a box of matches and a crumpled packet of fags from his pocket and stuffed one in his mouth.

"No time for that now" Ethan called to him from the back of the wagon. "There's still work to be done".

"Fuck off! I'll come when I'm ready".

He struck a match and sparked up muttering to himself and anybody else around that might be listening, "If he don't stop comin' the big I am, I swear I'm goin' to swing for him. Prick!"

Pyke, Jacko standing next to him, stood at the window in his office surveying the activity on the floor below. Before they left storage the contents of the wagons had been covered with green tarpaulin and now all looked the same. That way, when the wagon holding the artefacts was covered in the same canvas and placed amongst them it wouldn't look out of place and they would be free to load it onto the train without arousing suspicion. At least, that was the theory. The story.

Ethan came in and joined him at the window. "Mind if I make a suggestion" he volunteered cautiously after a moment.

"Oh aye, and what might that be?" Pyke replied in his usual off-hand manner.

"Before your assignment arrives, you dismiss all but your own men. You wouldn't want to arouse suspicion and jeopardise getting it away. Worse still, have one of them open their mouth after its gone and bring trouble to your door".

Pyke thought about it.

The truth was all Ethan wanted was to make sure anybody who wasn't a hardened felon and part of Pyke's brutal band of vicious thugs was out of the way, so they didn't get caught in the crossfire. No point risking harm coming to innocent people.

"Aye, you might be right" Pyke said before turning to Jacko. "See to it" he instructed bluntly.

CHAPTER 23

As darkness fell, the time had finally arrived for Pyke to receive his comeuppance. There was only one thing standing in the way; the wagon carrying the artefacts still hadn't arrived.

Ethan was starting to panic. If it didn't arrive before it was time to leave for the railroad, then the whole exercise would be rendered pointless. His mind was racing. Had Pyke somehow managed to get wind of what was about to happen? He wouldn't be surprised, around these parts, you couldn't take a crap without somebody knowing about it and shouting the joyful news from the rooftops. Or had the odious puppet master been playing them for fools all along? He didn't think so. Even so...

He needn't have worried.

By the time to give the order to move out had arrived, the innocent men had been dismissed and the cart finally rolled through the door.

"Swing it around over here" he had called to Frankie driving the cart, pointing to a gap in the column of several wagons already lined up ready to go.

Frankie guided the cart into the space left.

"Get it covered by the canvas" Ethan shouted, "And make sure its secure".

Somewhat fortuitously, at the very moment the train of wagons was about to depart for the railway yard, the clouds forming the ominous grey canopy above parted, and the moon made a glorious entrance, a giant glowing ball of colour set against the jet-black of the sky beyond the hillside. And silhouetted against this golden glow, there was movement. A line of men on horseback slowly appearing to sit in a line strung out across the hilltop.

The horsemen watched and waited in silence. Two cowboys in their cotton shirts and wool trousers, cowboy hats and scarves. An Argentinian Gaucho wearing a woollen poncho and a black bolero hat, a glint in his eye and a cheroot hanging from the corner of his mouth. A native Indian, his face daubed in full war paint, not for some ancestral religious reason or in the fervent belief that it held a magical power of protection, simply to bring fear to the hearts of his enemies – scare the shit out of them. And finally, not to be outdone, sitting right there at the head of the line was the great man himself, Buffalo Bill Cody dressed in his famous tassled jacket and mounted on his magnificent white steed.

Without speaking, Bill surveyed the canal basin spread out below them. Taking stock.

The murky waters of the canal swept around a patch of land creating a "U" shape, a single path and an iron bridge spanning the water, the only things preventing it from being an island. The dusty barges that were moored there were either loaded to the gunnels with coal, or simply sitting there empty.

The centre of the "U" was dominated by red brick buildings blackened by grime. There were chimney stacks built from the same red brick, black iron cranes, the arms of which clawed out over the thick soup, and all around the ground was scattered with boxes and soiled tubs. Then there was the open workshop housing furnaces, anvils, and other machinery that, for now, remained concealed in the darkness. And at the heart of all this, sat a derelict warehouse; the hovel that Pyke called home.

As the posse waited in silence, Joe arrived on horseback, Hindbuck riding beside him looking kind of ridiculous in his greatcoat and bowler hat. Cody shook his head with both disbelief and disgust at the sight.

As Joe pulled up his mount next to him, Cody snorted and demanded to know, "Where the hell have you been?"

"You know how it is, Colonel" Joe replied with a casual shrug of his shoulders, "When a man gets an itch and he needs to scratch it".

Cody hmphed, reached over and, much to Hindbuck's surprise, plucked the bowler from his head and handed it to one of the cowboys who exchanged it for his own ten-gallon hat.

Cody handed the hat to Hindbuck, "Here, put this on" he told him. "We can't have you riding into battle looking like a banker".

Pretty certain that he had said banker and not something more demeaning, Hindbuck planted the hat on his head. Cody looked down at the heavy, aging nag the awkward looking detective was sitting astride. "I didn't know you rode, Hindbuck" he said derisively.

"Learned when I was a lad growing up" Hindbuck replied with emphatic certainty, looking anything but certain as he shuffled his backside in the saddle.

"Would that be on a horse?" Cody asked not bothering to hide the sarcasm in his voice.

Hindbuck wasn't sure if he was joking or not. He didn't get the chance to find out, cut off by a voice that called from the end of the line, "Here they come now".

Looking down into the basin, there was movement inside the warehouse, little more than a passing glimpse of a wagon moving. But it was there, nevertheless.

"There's about thirty of 'em from what I understand" Hindbuck said informatively.

"Just the way I like it" Cody replied with unconcealed relish. "Outnumbered. Takes me back to a time when I was working for the U.S. Army during the Indian wars back in the seventies. Less than fifty of us were ambushed by more than a thousand Indians and came out unscathed without losing a man. Got a Medal of Honour for that one as I recall".

The Indian rolled his eyes at just how ludicrous the suggestion was, there was not a single man of his race, either dead or alive, that would ever have let that happened. Not in a million years. Hindbuck just shook his head and wondered if there had ever been a time when Cody didn't have a tale to tell.

The first wagon out was driven by Tommy. He hadn't gone but a few a yards who looked up the hillside and… "Fuck me"! he exclaimed, wide eyed and barely able to believe his eyes.

Screaming down the hill was the posse, yelling and shouting and whooping, and hollering as they galloped towards the bridge, Cody's mane of silver-grey hair billowing in the wind along with the tassels of his buckskin jacket, Hindbuck hanging onto his cowboy hat to stop it from blowing off.

Momentarily, Tommy was dumbstruck and rooted to his seat, wagons piling up behind him. He was snapped from his reverie by Ethan's authoritative voice shouting from inside, "Move it out. Get going out there".

"Fuck that" Tommy replied, tossing aside the horses reins. He slipped out of his seat and jumped down from the wagon. But by then the word had spread back inside and panicked thugs were piling out of the warehouse right behind him and he was almost trampled in the rush.

They raced along the path looking to escape, only to find their way blocked by two more Indians on horseback. Just the sight of them sitting there holding spears was enough to fill them with mortal dread and they stopped dead in their tracks, dumbstruck. The Indians, looking the part with their painted faces, raised their spears and started warbling. Panic set in, the men all but falling over one another as they turned and started for the bridge. But their escape was blocked that way too, the posse having arrived only moments earlier thundering across it.

Fearing for their lives, many of them headed back inside, others dove into the foul, polluted waters, and tried to swim across the canal, easy pickings for the men waiting for them.

The two Indians charged, flinging with their spears. One of them missed its target, the other buried itself deep in the shoulder of a fleeing thug bringing him down.

The cowboys twirled their hemp lassos over their heads, the swirling ropes dropping over the heads and arms of their targets and, as the rope was yanked tight, their victims came to a sudden stop, their legs flaying as they were lifted off the ground.

Hindbuck stumbled more than leapt from his mount, but once on firm ground, he fumbled for his truncheon, finally whipping it out and beating anybody and everybody who crossed his path with it.

One man came around the lead wagon, stopped dead in his tracks when he found himself face to face with the Gaucho. The Gaucho, the cheroot still dangling in the corner of his mouth and tossing his bolas from hand to hand, gave him a cheeky smile, "Hello senor" he said as he tweaked his eyebrows.

The man, wide eyed, mouth gaping and looking like he was about to soil himself, went to say something, but at the last moment just turned and ran in panic. Not that he got very far. The Gaucho twirled his bolas above his head, let fly and the heavily weighted ropes wrapped themselves around the man's ankles bringing him crashing to the ground in a cloud of coal dust.

All the time this was going on, Cody was right there in the middle of the action, sitting astride his white charger and barking out orders. "Coral them inside" he yelled. "Make sure none of them escapes".

He needn't have bothered wasting his breath, in disarray the men were already racing back inside.

The panicked men, none of them being too bright in the head, immediately realised their mistake when they found themselves trapped inside the warehouse, herded in there like wild horses shepherded into corrals made of wooden poles out on the prairie.

Having heard the commotion, Pyke stood at the window with Jacko, incredulous at what he was witnessing on the warehouse floor below. It was total chaos, shambolic as his men looked around for some place to go. There was none.

Pyke caught sight of Chalky shoving his way out. "I thought you were going to deal with him when you found out he was guilty?" he snarled.

"With everything else, I haven't got round to it" Jacko replied for once nervous.

"Oh, for fuck's sake! Do I have to do everything myself?" Pyke spat, spraying spittle over the window.

He turned to the corner. "Where's the dog?"

"It was going mad earlier, so one of the blokes took it for a walk".

"Took it for a walk? Pyke exploded. "It's a bloody guard dog, for Christ's sake. It's meant to be here to keep me safe, not to go for bloody walkies whenever it feels like it".

Down in the warehouse, Ethan was in a fist fight with three of Pyke's army who, having realised his betrayal, had turned on him.

Pyke came out of his lair with Jacko and shuffled down the stairs. At the foot, Jacko attempted to clear a way through the crowd.

Over the shoulders of his assailants, Ethan could make out Pyke yelling "Shift... out'f my way... you'll pay for this, let me through" at anyone in his way.

But the men were having none of it, for once Pyke wasn't their main concern, his threats meant nothing.

Outside, Penny arrived with a horse drawn Black Maria - a closed, horse-drawn carriage with small windows on each side, a porched seat at the front and four wheels, two larger ones at the rear, two smaller ones at the front. On the sides, written in gold letters was the name of the force - to witness Cody's colourful army amidst a sea of broken, unconscious bodies. Picking off the stragglers who hadn't made it back inside. Fighting hand to hand. Cowboys with their fists, native Indians beating folks over the head with the blunt end of their tomahawks, and the Gaucho, a constant smile of his face, clearly having fun as he brought people down with his bolas and long whip.

It was mesmerising, just as Penny imagined it to be when he was sitting at home at night in front of the fire reading the novels of Mister Buntline while his mother cooked dinner. What wasn't written anywhere in Mister Buntline's paperbacks, was a man jumping onto the front of the Maria and trying to wrest the horse's reins from him.

Penny fumbled for his truncheon, found it, and started to beat the man around the shoulders and head with it. But the man was bigger and stronger and soon overpowered him. He took Penny by the shoulders and flung him to the ground, his head striking the side of the carriage on his way down. The man grabbed the reins, about to slap them when... he gasped, eyes wide as a lance speared into him, seeming to hang there before crashing to the ground right next to Penny.

Ethan disposed of the three men without much difficulty and started after Pyke who was making slow progress. Then, just before Ethan reached him, Pyke stopped and looked back. He was between a rock and a hard place, stranded between the young cowboy and Hindbuck, the guardian of the law, who stood his ground between him and the wide doors to freedom.

Pyke was snapped in a trap like the disgusting, infectious rodent that he was.

His shallow wheeze rasped, and he struggled to breathe. Fatty sweat poured out of every pore. From his brow. Dribbling down his cheek, over his lips, over his chin and dripping onto the floor.

"You'll pay for this. Both of you" he declared defiantly, licking the sweat from his lips. He turned to Jacko. But Jacko was not there. Already gone.

In that brief moment, Pyke realised his oppressive reign was finally over. He closed his eyes, his shoulders slumped, and he gave a heavy, wretched sigh of defeat.

When Jacko came running out of the warehouse, he immediately spotted Chalky scrambling up the bank on the far side of the canal having swum across to the other side. And it seemed his loyalty ran deeper than his cowardice. Remembering Pyke's order to him, he took a pistol from his pocket, fired a single shot and...

Chalky tumbled back down the bank and into the water with a splash that sent ripples across its dark and putrid surface. Dead as a doornail in one of the nail shops back in the town.

The barrel of the pistol was still smoking when the gaucho's whip wrapped around Jacko's wrist and whisked it away. Jacko turned to look, gobsmacked when he saw the Gaucho, still chewing on the cheroot hanging from the corner of his mouth, grinning back at him.

With the artefacts recovered and Pyke taken into custody, his cronies, realising any resistance was futile, started singing like canaries in their cages in the underground mines, already pleading their cases and vowing to give evidence against him in the hope of winning a lesser sentence. Surprisingly, the one singing the loudest was the one with the most to sing about, Jacko.

Still wearing the cowboy's hat and with his hands dug deep in the pockets of his greatcoat, Hindbuck ambled over to join Penny who was standing next to the Maria nursing a gash over his eye with a handkerchief. He arrived just as Pyke and Jacko, their hands handcuffed behind their backs, were being loaded into the back of the black police wagon by Joe and one of the cowboys.

The subservient Jacko meekly did as he was told, climbed the steps, and disappeared into the back of the carriage without protest, Pyke on the other hand was far less cooperative.

"Get your filthy hands off me you fuckin' savage" he snarled, shrugging off Joe's helping hand before the half-breed gave him a swift kick on the backside.

Pyke stumbled into the back of the maria and Joe slammed the door shut. Pyke flopped down on one of the wooden benches on either side of the cab, glaring venomously at Jacko sitting meekly opposite him. Then he turned to peer out through one of the small windows and found Hindbuck staring back at him.

"This ain't over yet, Hindbuck. You mark my words, I ain't finished with you yet", he declared defiantly, although he had little to be defiant about.

Hindbuck, remained unconcerned, with Jacko's testimony, it seemed unlikely the fat man would ever see the light of day again.

Cody came out of the warehouse and walked across the yard carrying Hindbuck's bowler hat.

Hindbuck turned his attention to Penny standing next to him still dabbing the gash over his eye with his handkerchief, fresh blood trickling down his check.

"What was the last thing I said to you?" Hindbuck snapped with angered concern, "Come in late. Come in at the last minute and avoid trouble. That's what I said. And what do you do? You come charging in all guns blazing and... just look at the state of you?"

"I'm fine, sir. Honestly. Just a bang on the head, that's all" Penny assured him, wearing the injury like it was a badge of honour. "You never know, it might've knocked some sense in".

Hindbuck gritted his teeth.

Penny quickly apologised, embarrassed by his own smart Alec comment, "Sorry, sir" he said sheepishly.

Hindbuck's eyes softened and he started to smile, "No need to be sorry, son", he told him fondly. Then he watched as Penny, still holding the handkerchief to his head, crossed to the maria climbed up onto the hard, wooden seat up front and grabbed the reins.

"I thought you might like this back" Cody said handing Hindbuck his bowler.

"Thanks, Colonel" Hindbuck replied as he took the hat and gave him the one borrowed from the cowboy in exchange, all the time distracted, looking around. All he could see were Cody's men rounding up the thugs and loading them onto the back of the wagons. Mopping up. In truth, the whole thing had been a non-event, over almost before it began. Faced with what they perceived as painted savages and marauding cowboys, their minds

214

instantly springing to the tales of Ned Buntline where an armful of cavalry officers fought off an army of thousands, they had panicked and, once Pyke was taken, that was it. Game over.

"Are you alright, Hindbuck?" Cody asked registering the detective's distraction.

"Have you seen Ethan" Hindbuck asked distantly, his eyes continuing to search.

"Last I heard, he'd grabbed one of the horses and headed off to see young Ella in the infirmary"

"Shit!" Hindbuck exclaimed.

"Is there a problem with that? Cody asked looking confused.

"You could say that. Ella died earlier this evening. The beating she took ruptured her insides and... I only heard just before I left the station".

"I'm sorry".

"Me too. Thing is, once Ethan gets to the infirmary and finds out, I know exactly where he'll be headed. And it spells trouble. Big trouble".

"In that case, we have to stop him".

With that, the two men headed for their mounts. Hindbuck called to Penny who was about the pull away in the maria, "Drop them off and bring the maria to the factory behind the pub. We might need it".

"Take one of the other horses, it'll be morning before that old nag of yours gets you there" Cody told him.

One of the cowboys handed Hindbuck the reins to his pony and Hindbuck mounted up. He looked across to see Cody tug on the reins of his white horse and wheel around… and a moment later they were on their way.

The horses hooves clattered on the bridge as they crossed over it and galloped up the hill on the far side of the canal. Two shrinking silhouettes disappearing into the heart of a glowing moon filling the night sky.

CHAPTER 24

Hearing the clip-clop of horses hooves galloping over cobbled stones, folks rushed out of their front doors and the narrow alleyways of their terraced cottages to see what all the fuss was about, watching in awed disbelief as Ethan, head down low over his pony's neck, raced past.

As he neared the corner of the street, he deftly turned the pony's head and a moment later disappeared into the alleyway at the side of the pub.

The townsfolk started to return to their homes, still buoyed by the once in a lifetime experience of having seen a real-life cowboy riding through the streets of the Black Country. But the excitement wasn't over yet.

Hearing a distant sound, they turned and looked down the street towards the bridge over the canal that marked the start of the town. At first, there was nothing but a distant echo that grew steadily louder. Then, as if they were nothing more than a ghostly apparition emerging from the ether, Hindbuck and Cody appeared riding over the bridge towards them

The townsfolk watched gobsmacked as they galloped past. "That's Mister Hindbuck, isn't it?" a woman standing on the pavement with her arms folded asked of her husband standing next to her. "I didn't know he could ride".

"Don't look like he can to me" the man replied dryly.

And he was right, Hindbuck was not so much riding the pony as he was being carried by it, his head hanging around the animal's neck as it dutifully followed Cody up front. Like it knew it had a part to play.

Cody, on the other hand, ever the consummate showman, straightened his back, took off his hat and waved it playing to the crowd... and they loved it, clapping, and cheering to a man... and a woman.

Ethan had already emerged from the alleyway and his mount was kicking up clouds of dust as he galloped across the flattened path of compacted, ebony coal dust towards the squalid factory building silhouetted against the obligatory blood-red of the night sky.

The jungle drums had sounded loud and clear and already men in their work clothes were appearing from everywhere, running behind him, climbing over fences, and sliding down the hills of charred cinders and spoil. Kicking up even more clouds of coal dust as they raced to get to the factory on time.

Ethan didn't wait to dismount when he reached the factory door, he just kept his head down and charged through. The handful of men that were already gathered there stunned, stepped back as he carved his way through.

When he reached the makeshift ring, Pyke's chair sitting there empty, Nobby was already there, his back to him as he talked to another man. And as Ethan pulled up his mount, lifted his leg over the pony's head and slid to the ground, handed the reins to a man standing nearby

Nobby turned and glared at him. "I didn't expect to see you here ever again" he said spitting his scorn. "Bit dangerous, don't you think?"

"For you maybe, not for me" Ethan replied steely eyed and focused.

Nobby laughed mockingly, derisively, "Hear that, lads. I think the ponce has come here looking for a fight.

Ethan didn't flinch.

"Do you think he's up to it?"

A murmur spread amongst the crowd.

"Is that the best you've got to offer? Ethan asked matching the other man's scorn. "Empty words. I thought you were supposed to be harder than that?".

Nobby jabbed his finger in Ethan's face "Look here, I don't take kindly to folks taking the piss. Don't like folks waltzing in here coming the big 'I am' throwing their weight around. Making demands. So, if you've got any sense, you'll just turn around and…"

"Are we going to settle this like men, or just stand here like little old ladies gossiping all night?"

Nobby fixed him in the eye. "All right, you want a fight, you got one".

Ethan didn't flinch from his brutish glare.

"One of you lads pop down the undertakers, will you?" Nobby called to the crowd, to no one in particular. "Make sure he's not busy. He's goin' to be needed here to pick up the pieces when I'm done".

Ethan still didn't flinch.

Nobby slipped his braces off his shoulders. "I should've finished you off the last time instead'f just putting you in hospital... how're your ribs, by the way?"

Ethan felt the muscles in his stomach tighten and his fists clenched. But he still didn't react.

What was at first a modest crowd was fast becoming a mass of maggots in a can, men appearing from everywhere. They crowded around the makeshift ring, climbed up the steel girders into the dusty ceiling to get a better sight of the action and never stopped shouting their wagers as they jostled noisily around the bookie who must have thought all his Christmases had come at once.

"A bob on Nobby".

"A tanner on Nobby".

"Threepence on the cowboy".

Everybody stopped and looked at the source of the latest wager, a man they all referred to as 'Mad Charlie', whether to his face or not. It didn't really matter.

"You do realise Nobby's hard as nails. A fighter and the kid's only just out of nappies?" one of them asked.

Mad Charlie didn't seem to care and shrugged hopefully "Well, you never know".

The other men weren't convinced. They shook their heads in disbelief and turned back to the bookie. "A tanner says Nobby stops him inside five minutes" one of them said.

"A bob says it's more like three" said another.

"Alright, Alright" the Bookie shouted over a sea of hands thrusting money at him. "Quieten down, you'll all get your turn".

Nobby took off his collarless shirt, while Ethan took off his hat and Slicker and handed them to one of the men standing closest to the ring.

Neither man took their steely eyes off one another.

"Out of the way. Coming through" Hindbuck was heard to shout over the clatter of horse's hooves.

Charging in from outside, Hindbuck was carried in on his pony, the crowd parting as he ploughed right through them, all the time waving them aside, "Move it... Out of the way... Move it..."

Cody was only a length behind him, and as the pony pulled up just short of the ring and Hindbuck slid from the saddle, he leapt from his white mount and placed his arm across him to prevent the policeman from moving closer.

Hindbuck fixed him in the eye.

"Leave it" Cody told him quietly. "If he walks away now, he'll never forgive himself... or you"

Hindbuck stood conflicted, not moving.

Cody continued to stare at him, then nodded and slowly lowered his arm.

As Ethan and Nobby warily circled one another, sized one another up, before making their move, the hush that fell was palpable.

Ethan eyed Nobby up and down. He was probably a good four stone heavier than the younger man but had muscles that were toned from all the years he had fought bare fisted and undefeated. Under normal circumstances it would not have been a fair fight, but these were not normal circumstances and Nobby's weak spot, the flabby beer belly hanging over his belt, would give him an advantage Ethan thought. The other man didn't think anything, he just wanted to get on with it.

Nobby sneered as he leaned forward and stuck out his chin, "Go on then, give it your best shot pretty boy" he taunted.

Ethan flicked out his fist and Nobby pulled his chin back in plenty of time.

"Close, but no cigar" Nobby sneered as he turned to the crowd. "Looks like this is goin' to be a piece of cake" he smirked.

Round and round they went, neither throwing a punch or flinching from the resolute and unwavering eyes of the other. Mumblings rose from the crowd who had started to get impatient and Nobby started to become edgy and irritable. Exasperated. It was just the way Ethan wanted it to be. A man who wasn't in control of his emotions, wasn't in control of anything.

"Are we goin' to fight, or what?" Nobby complained bitterly. "Or shall I get somebody to fetch your ballet shoes?"

Ethan ignored his jibe and continued to circle. And all the time Nobby was becoming more irascible and the crowd more and more unsettled. They started to boo and jeer and wave their hands in disgust.

"Get on with it", one of them called before some of the others joined in.

"I thought you cowboys were hard nuts"

"What are you, a man or a mouse?"

"Pussy"

Hindbuck looked to Cody, who shrugged his shoulders, and frowned quizzically. "More than one way to skin a rabbit" the Colonel assured him.

Finally, with frustration getting the better of him, Nobby had had enough pissing about and threw the first punch, a right hook that flew way over Ethan's head as he deftly ducked under it.

Nobby threw another punch, a left this time, but the result was the same. Enraged, he started throwing punches willy-nilly one after the other. A left, a right, left, right and... and all time Ethan dodged the lumbering onslaught, ducking and diving, floating like he was some kind of dainty, coloured insect on the wing.

Nobby's rage was starting to consume him. And when it did, then, and only then, did Ethan make his move. As Nobby shambled forward ready to throw yet another punch, Ethan got in first with one of his own, a straight right that split Nobby's nose and splattered blood over the faces of those crowded around him.

Momentarily, Nobby started to sway. Then he blinked, composed himself and the fight was on... and the crowd's jeers turned to loud and enthusiastic cheers.

Ethan continued to dance as the bigger man rained punches down on him. And while he was on the receiving end of many of them and only threw in the odd shot of his own, he spent most of the time defending himself as the bigger man targeted his ribs, knowing full well that they were already weak and still not fully mended.

A glancing blow caught Ethan on the side of his head spinning him around, and Nobby moved in for the kill. Too soon, his frustration getting the better of him.

For the second time, Ethan caught him in the face with a straight right. But this time it had little effect, Nobby simply swatting away the blood from his nose and hit Ethan full in the face with a punch of his own. And now the two men were exchanging blows one after another, the boisterous crowd urging them on as they slugged it out.

A right to his kidney and a left to his belly left Ethan reeling. But he tried not to show it and threw a left of his own which Nobby swatted away contemptuously.

A right... and Nobby blocked that too.

A left to Ethan's face spit his nose wide open and saw the fight turning Nobby's way, the brute going in for the kill.

A left, Ethan blocked it

A right and Ethan blocked that too.

Punches were raining down on him faster and faster and while with the help of his deft footwork and agility he defended most of them, others reached their target. A left to the jaw, a right to the kidneys. An uppercut to the jaw, a blow to his ribs. But they were enraged blows driven by Nobby's frustration leaving him unprotected. He was out of control and Ethan was there waiting to take advantage.

As Nobby moved in to cement his advantage, Ethan took his opportunity and caught him with a straight left followed immediately by an uppercut to the jaw. The big man reeled, still reeling when Ethan threw a right cross that spun Nobby's head one way, and a left that spun it the other. An uppercut to his belly swiftly followed by a second had Nobby gasping, staggering.

And that was when Ethan made his mistake.

He stepped back waiting for the other man to recover sufficiently for him to inflict still more pain on him rather than forcing home his advantage, willing him to bring the fight to him so that he could take revenge for every tortured year of abuse and depravity he had forced Ella, the daughter he was supposed to protect, to endure.

Still groggy, Nobby lumbered forward and Ethan made his move. But by then Nobby had determined to play dirty and an agonising kick in his balls saw Ethan drop to his knees, the penetrating pain excruciating.

The hum of the crowd turned to stony silence as he turned away to one side and threw up.

Clouds of dust kicked up by the horses hooves and the wheels of the maria drifted away as the police wagon raced across the open ground between the rear of the pub and the factory. Outside the wide doors, Penny pulled up, leapt down from the covered cab and raced inside.

Nobby stood over Ethan and looked down at him still on his knees. "And you thought you could just waltz in here and put the world to rights" he scoffed with vile contempt. "Like I once told you, things don't happen that way round here... and now you're goin' to see how those what thinks otherwise have to pay".

The Colonel and Hindbuck made to move in to prevent any more bloodshed, but as they did, so something totally unexpected happened.

As Nobby moved in to finish things off, driven by all the years of oppression, the crowd surged forward and surged into the ring. It was chaos, mayhem. Nobby was surrounded by men holding him back and giving him a sly one in the kidneys while they were at it, while others lifted Ethan to his feet and slapped him around the face. One of them even tipped water from a bucket over his head to bring him round.

As the crowd retreated from the ring, one of them muttered quietly to Ethan, "Go on, lad. Finish him off and do us all a favour".

From that moment on, and with Nobby still groggy, Ethan went on the offensive, raining punches aimed to inflict the most damage. Not that he had it all his own way, Nobby threw a few punches of his own, most of which Ethan either dodged with his guile and weakened agility or blocked without them reaching their target and causing any real harm. A final blow to the belly and an uppercut to the jaw saw the fight ended and Nobby drop to his knees.

As Ethan stood over him, Nobby's eyes were glazed over and he swayed back and forth... before finally he fell flat on his face in the dust and dirt at Ethan's feet.

The crowd went wild, surging into the ring to congratulate him, shaking his hand, and slapping him on the back. It was all Cody and Hindbuck could do to force their way through and get to him.

Hindbuck stood outside the factory with Cody and Ethan, watching as Penny supervised the men loading the unconscious Nobby onto the Maria.

"You'd better get yourself checked out, make sure there's no damage to those ribs of yours" Cody told Ethan leaving no room for argument.

Hindbuck called over to Penny, "Get him over to the infirmary, and while you're there, charge him with affray, actual bodily harm and anything else you can think of while you're at it".

"Right you are, Inspector" Penny replied with new-found confidence, the trust the inspector had put in him by allowing to escort Nobby unsupervised not having gone unnoticed. He slammed the rear door of the maria shut and locked it up. Went around to the cab and climbed on up.

A moment later, Hindbuck was watching as the carriage headed across the desolate ground towards the town.

CHAPTER 25

Despite the lateness of the hour, the pub was still very much open for business. Light filtered through its etched, frosted windows and spilled across the pavement outside, and the enthusiastic tinkling of the old joanna accompanied the sound of townsfolk equally enthusiastically belting out some of the most popular songs of the day, *'Down at the Old Bull and Bush'*, *'Goodbye Dolly Grey'*, and *'Any Old Iron'*.

The bar was crowded and noisy, people having to shout to be heard. The piano player was over in the corner where he could usually be found, Hindbuck was standing next to the bar with Ethan, listening as best he could to Cody regaling his adoring admirers with outlandish tales of daring, and Penny was sitting at one of the tables with two of the local girls, one on his knee, the other sitting beside him. Both of them were pretty and wore their hair loose. One of them, the girl sitting on his knee, the girl who had been serving behind the bar when Ethan first arrived, was wearing his helmet.

228

Behind the bar, Nell was rushed off her feet pulling beer and serving impatient customers, "Alright, alright", she shouted as loud as she could, "Wait your turn. There's plenty for everybody".

"It was quite a sight" Penny enthused, his face flushed, only on this occasion it was far from a sign of him being embarrassed, "they came screaming down the hill and started rounding people up. That's when I came in with the maria".

The girl sitting on his knee stroked his hair, "You must be so brave" she cooed.

"Well, you know" Penny replied as casually as he could muster, all part of the job.

"Oi you, get your arse over here and do what you're paid to do" Nell yelled from the bar.

The young woman sitting on Penny's knee sighed and rolled her shoulders "Do what your paid to do" she mimicked, taking the hat off, and plonking it on the other girl's head before getting up and stropping towards the bar. The other girl was up and sitting on Penny's knee in a flash. She ran her fingers through his hair.

"Do you want to walk out with me some time?" she asked licking her lips enticingly, her husky tone suggesting she had more than a gentle stroll on her mind.

Penny was in heaven, the boy fast becoming a man.

"We were heavily outnumbered" Cody maintained taking a sip of his whiskey before continuing. "More than three thousand of the painted Indians and just fifty of us... and we came out unscathed without losing a man. Didn't harm a hair on our heads". He reflected a moment. "Got a Medal of Honour for that one from what I recall".

"Where did the extra two thousand come from since earlier" Hindbuck asked Ethan with a wry smile.

"It was five hundred when I first heard him tell it" Ethan replied with a tip of his head. "And as for the Medal of Honour, what he's never going to tell you is that it was later rescinded. Seems it's an honour reserved for military personnel not civilians and they wouldn't change the rules, not even for the Colonel".

Hindbuck was suddenly distracted. "Uh, uh. Here comes trouble" he said with a sigh.

The Chief Constable had just come in and was standing just inside the door looking around for the insubordinate police officer. Unfortunately, he caught sight of him before Hindbuck had chance to slip away and, with gritted teeth, he glared at him nodding his head outside. Then he went out again.

"I may be some time" Hindbuck said drolly.

Ethan just smiled, and from the end of the bar, Cody caught sight of Hindbuck shoving his way through the crowd on his way out to receive his dressing down.

The Chief Constable was pacing up and down on the pavement outside the pub like a coiled spring when Hindbuck came out to join him.

"You wanted to see me, sir" Hindbuck asked brightly like he was passing the time of day.

The Chief glared at him contemptuously. "My God, you've done it this time, Hindbuck. This really does take

230

the biscuit" he spat barely able to control his anger. "I should have you arrested".

"For what?"

"Initiating a disturbance, perpetuating a riot, affray, causing actual bodily harm and… and now you have the effrontery to be seen sanctioning a lock in at the local hostelry. It's just not on".

"Ah, there you are, the man I was looking for".

Cody had come out behind them and was standing on the pavement between them and the door to the pub.

"I just wanted to say thank you and to shake your hand" he said offering the Chief his hand.

The Chief took it warily. Confused. "Thank me?"

"For organising this little shindig. When I heard what you'd arranged, I've gotta say I was mightily impressed. It's not often a man's so gracious as to show his appreciation so generously".

"Yes… yes, well you know how it is" the Chief backtracked ingratiating himself, "just a small token, that's all. Not nearly enough, I'd say. Thank you".

"The least I could do. When Hindbuck here told me the trouble you were having with that man Pyke and how short-handed you were, I was only too glad to step in and lend a hand. The least a man can do in order to maintain strong international relations, don't you think?"

"Yes. Quite" the Chief squirmed.

"In that case, I'll head back inside while you heap praise on this man here" he slapped Hindbuck on the back. "Wouldn't want to embarrass him".

"Yes. Right… Well thank you again".

"My pleasure" Cody replied, winking at Hindbuck before sauntering back inside.

The Chief stood for a few moments, wanting to say something more but feeling he couldn't, his subordinate having backed him into a corner and done him like a kipper. "Right. Well, I'll be off then, Hindbuck" he finally managed. "I'll see you at the station tomorrow".

Hindbuck let him walk away before calling after him, "Haven't you forgotten something?"

The Chief turned back.

"I'm on holiday tomorrow and after that I'll be heading off into the sunset. Remember?"

"Ah yes. Right" the Chief replied, the words sticking in his throat as he spoke, "Good luck then".

And with that he walked to his carriage which was waiting just along next to the pavement, climbed aboard, slammed the door shut and moments later the carriage was disappearing into the drifting smoke shrouding the end of the street.

Hindbuck smiled and shook his head... and went back inside to re-join the party.

"I just wanted to thank you" Ethan said with sincerity as he stood at the end of the bar with Nell.

"For what?"

"Everything. Looking out for me. Taking good care. Nursing me. Feeding me until I was fit to burst".

"Nonsense, it's me that should be thanking you" Nell told him. "You and Mister Cody. We all should"

Ethan's eyes narrowed questioningly.

Nell nodded back over her shoulder into the room, "Just look at em', singing, laughing, and joking. They're good people, the folks from the Black Country, hardworking, honest, God fearing and with a caustic sense of humour. All right, not everybody might get it, but it's there all the same. It's just that while that vile pig of a man was around, they forgot to remember it, that's all. And you helped 'em remember".

Ethan took a moment to let her words sink in.

"Now, come here you great lummox and give me a hug".

She threw her arms around him and pulled him tight. Not knowing her own strength, Ethan felt his ribs crack and excruciating pain surged through his body. But he didn't say anything. How could he?

With Nell still crushing him a bear hug, an expectant hush fell over the room, as one of the men dressed in his baggies and collarless shirt, climbed up onto a table and began to sing '*A Bird in Gilded Cage*' unaccompanied. His voice was sweet and clear, and it was a fitting end to what had been an eventful day, and an even more eventful night.

Ella's funeral took place a few days later. Ethan and Cody had stayed on and were in attendance along with Hindbuck, Penny and many of the townsfolk. Reverend Price eulogised with warm words of comfort, and it was almost as though Ella's passing represented the end of a dark era. A time when tyranny ruled, and hope was just a fleeting dream.

The following morning, it was time for Ethan and Cody to leave the Black Country for one last time, and Hindbuck and Penny were there at the railway station to see them off.

"So, what now, *Mister* Hindbuck? Where do you go from here?" Cody asked as they stood on the platform.

"I haven't figured that one out yet" Hindbuck told him. "Somewhere you can breathe the air preferably".

"Out west. The Great Plains, perhaps?"

Hindbuck raised his eyebrows.

"I'm serious" Cody assured him. "You could come work for me, I could do with a new head of security… and good men are hard to come by".

Hindbuck gave a wry smile and then laughed out loud. The idea was preposterous… but then again.

Ethan was distracted and kept looking around. It was as though he was expecting a passing cloud of steam to billow over the platform and when it dissipated to see Ella standing there. But it never happened. She never came.

A horn sounded and moments later a train pulled into the station and stopped alongside the platform.

Cody shook Hindbuck's hand, "Whatever happens in the future, it's been one hell of a swansong. Not quite what I'd imagined my final hurrah to be, but fitting, nonetheless".

Hindbuck nodded.

Cody turned to Penny. "You did all right, son. Keep up the good work" he told him warmly with a wink.

And with that, the ebullient entertainer strode off across the platform towards the train.

As Ethan bade them farewell, Penny couldn't stop grinning. Mister Cody, the Colonel... Buffalo Bill, had told him he did all right. "*I wonder if I'll turn up in one of Mister Buntline's stories?*" he thought to himself swelling with pride. It seemed he hadn't quite grown up just yet.

Cody was about to climb the steps into the carriage when Hindbuck called to him "Colonel".

Cody turned back and looked.

"How many men was it we defeated again?"

"Couldn't rightly tell. Three, four hundred... maybe more". And with that, he threw back his head, guffawed loudly, and with an overly theatrical wave of his hand, boarded the train.

Standing at the foot of the carriage steps, his saddlebag slung over his shoulder, Ethan continued to wait, his eyes searching for.... whatever it was he was searching for. Waiting for.

"All aboard" came the call.

There was a loud hiss as the pressure was released and steam billowed from under the engine to engulf him. And as it drifted away, Hindbuck watched as, inside the carriage, he made his way down the aisle and flopped disconsolately into his seat by the window.

The train's whistle sounded.

As the train pulled away, Ethan sat up sharply.

Nell had arrived. Appearing from under the arched entrance, and bustling past Hindbuck and Penny as she hurried across the platform towards the train. She was clinging for dear life onto a brown paper wrapped package tucked under her arm. Like it was fragile, and she was afraid to let go.

Ethan was up in a flash.

Cody, who had been seated opposite Ethan reading a newspaper, looked, and watched as he raced up the aisle.

At the rear of the carriage, Ethan pulled down the window. Out on the platform, barely able to keep up, Nell trotted alongside the moving train. She handed him the package through the open window.

"How did you get it?" Ethan asked as he took it.

"Don't ask" Nell replied breathlessly, "just you take good care of it, that's".

"I will, Nell. You have my word".

Her job done, Nell stopped running and stood with her hands on her hips, breathing heavily as she watched the train ever so slowly disappear into the distance. Only when it was gone did she take a deep breath, exhale, and head back towards the exit.

"That was close" she decreed breathlessly as she passed Hindbuck and Penny.

Hindbuck turned and watched her go. "Hope it keeps hot" Hindbuck called to her, remembering all the times Ethan had complained that Nell didn't know how much stew was enough.

"Not too hot I hope" Nell chuckled as she disappeared under the arch.

Hindbuck wrinkled his brow, wondering what the hell that was supposed to mean. He turned to Penny and slapped him on the back. "Come on, lad. Let's get out'f here" he said.

And they walked away together, Hindbuck towards a well-earned retirement, and Penny towards his future… whatever that might hold in store for him.

CHAPTER 26

With the tour finally over, Ethan returned to his homeland and on his arrival, he simply couldn't wait to saddle up and take a ride in the crisp, clean air of America's fall. So he slung the saddlebag he had carried with him all the time he had been away over his favourite pony's back, slipped his foot into the stirrup, mounted up and was soon heading out into the wild.

The distant horizon was dominated by snow-capped mountains so high they almost touched the fluffy white clouds drifting in the clear blue sky, and as Ethan rode across the open plains with the wind blowing in his face, it was good to be home, good to breathe fresh, clean air again.

As the surefooted the pony carried him over the bunchgrass scattered in clumps over the ground, way off in the distance he could just about make out a couple of grazing bison, the symbol of the west. Sadly, it was an increasingly rare sight, the bison population having been all but wiped out by the over hunting and indiscriminate slaughter Cody himself had been partially responsible for.

Approaching the foothills, the bunchgrass thinned.

Once in the foothills, Ethan guided the pony onto a narrow track that rose high towards the summit. Before long he came to a stream that flowed crystal clear as it meandered its way back down to the steppes below.

He pulled up his mount, dismounted and left the pony happily munching on a small bush before making his way to the water's edge. And as he sat on a boulder at the side of the stream, he quietly reminisced, remembering the young woman that had made such an impression on him.

After a while, he started to smile to himself…

Reverend Price had been incandescent. "Over my dead body. It's the work of the devil" he had raged… until someone reminded him that the best-known mention of cremation was in the Book of Genesis when God had ordered Abraham to prepared a funeral pyre for the sacrifice of his son, Isaac". Even then the Reverend had still not been totally convinced, cremation in its present form hadn't been around much more than a quarter of a century and it was simply not something that happened in the Methodist Chapel. Not then.

"When they're dead, folks are buried in the ground along with everybody else" he had insisted. "Besides, who's going to pay for it?".

Of course, all the Reverend's objections quickly dissolved away when Cody offered to foot the bill and throw in a donation to the chapel fund along with it.

Ethan stood up, strode to his pony, lifted down the saddlebag and carried it back to the boulder. Sitting back down again, he opened up the saddlebag and from it he took the package that Nell had handed to him just before he had left, and that he had carried with him ever since.

He carefully untied the string that held it tight and unwrapped the brown paper. Inside there was an urn, and as he stared at it sitting in his hands, he wondered how Nell had managed to get hold of it, and just what it was that someone was now holding onto in a mistaken belief.

He got to his feet and slowly walked over to the edge of the stream, pausing a moment to gaze at the crystal-clear water swirling around the smooth stones lying on its sandy bed. Then he dropped to his haunches, scooped up a handful of the water and took a drink, taking one last look around as he did so.

Rising to his feet, he shook the water from his hand. Gently he kissed the urn. Then, carefully, he unscrewed it's lid, hesitating before finally tipping Ella's ashes into the fast-flowing stream before they were carried away towards their final resting place.

As he watched the ashes floating away on the surface of the water, he reflected on what might have been. When he had first arrived in the Black Country to retrieve the Colonel's treasured possessions, he couldn't wait get out of there, to leave the hellish place as soon as humanly possible and never to return. Why would anyone in their right mind willingly stay there? Everything single thing was dusty and oppressive. Building were crammed together so tightly it felt as though they were about to tumble in on one another, and the ground constantly shook from the heavy industry carried out there. The smoke-filled skies burned with flame and the air was so dense and putrid you could hardly breath.

And yet, despite all this, despite all the oppression and hardship they were forced to endure, the folks who lived there, just like Nell had said, were God fearing, down to earth folk who accepted their lot in life with a casual shrug of their shoulders and went about their lives without complaint. Those were the cards they were dealt, and they had no choice other than to play them. Life goes on.

As Ella's ashes were slowly dispersed before finally disappearing forever, Ethan remembered with heartache the young woman who had changed his life so profoundly, and one of the last things he had said to her as she lay in the infirmary bed waiting to draw her last breath…

"One day I will take you there, I promise. You have my word on it".

ABOUT THE AUTHOR

Michael lives with his wife, Susan, close to an Area of Outstanding Natural Beauty in central England.

After working in the film and television industry, both in the UK and Australia, he later became Head of Media and a lecturer in film and television production at college and university. But his passion has always been writing, initially drama and humorous scripts for the screen, more recently novels.

Other titles (humour) writing as Tez Foster:

No, Not Really

For more information:

Email: mtfoster@btinternet.com

Website: www.tezfoster.co.uk

Printed in Great Britain
by Amazon

47022838R00149